Other Books by Mark Beauregard

Novels

Blood & Chocolate

The Scarlet Dove

Give the Drummer Some

The Whale: A Love Story

Other Novels in this Series

The French Art of Stealing

THE FRENCH ART
OF REVENGE

THE FRENCH ART
OF REVENGE

a novel by

Mark Beauregard

A GIANT BOOK

Second GIANT PUBLISHING EDITION January 2019

Bibliographical Note: This novel is an unabridged reprint of the same novel published in 2014 under the name Mark Zero. Mark Zero and Mark Beauregard are both pen names of Beauregard Mark Zero. First Giant Publishing Edition August 2014.

THIS BOOK IS A WORK OF FICTION. CHARACTERS, PLACES AND INCIDENTS ARE THE PRODUCTS OF THE AUTHOR'S IMAGINATION, AND ANY REAL NAMES OR LOCALES USED IN THIS BOOK ARE USED FICTITIOUSLY.

Published in the United States of America by Giant Publishing,

Tucson, Arizona.

Library of Congress Control Number: 2019932910

ISBN-13: 978-1-933975-12-2

10 9 8 7 6 5 4 3

cover images:
Max Beckman, *Self-Portrait Dressed as a Clown*, 1921.
Gustave Caillebotte, *Self-Portrait*, circa 1895.
Martial Colomb, Photograph of the Grand Palais in Snow, Paris, 2010.
All images used by permission.

WWW.GIANTPUBLISHING.COM

Contents

I

The Despair of Pierrot

On the morning after the daring theft of a priceless James Ensor painting from the Grand Palais in Paris, I was allowed to leave the Les Halles Police Station after only a few hours of questioning. The fact that I had provided no clues about the disappearance of *The Despair of Pierrot* made me seem, in the eyes of the police, merely clever—they did not even have sufficient evidence to hold me—but they were convinced that I was guilty, so I was equally convinced, as I walked back to my apartment in the Marais, that plain-clothes detectives were somewhere on the street behind me, watching for my first mistake. However, I knew something that the police did not know: that the real thief had not stolen the painting for any of the usual motives. This was a crime of passion, but unlike most crimes of passion, it had been meticulously and diabolically well-planned.

My name is Luke Johnson, and I'm an American war photographer based in Paris. Why I was accused of stealing *The Despair of Pierrot* is a complicated story, which begins with the equally complicated story of how Yves Saint Laurent's longtime lover Pierre Bergé tried to kill me. That story, in turn, began while I was the guest of honor at a fancy dinner party at one of the most exclusive art galleries in the world, on the Champs-Élysées—and why, you might ask, was an American war photographer being celebrated by the wealthiest people in France in one of the most exclusive art galleries in the world?

The final police reports explained some of these things but

1

could not account for the true motives behind one of the most public art heists in recent memory. So let's begin somewhere near the beginning, at that dinner party on the Champs-Élysées, where Pierre Bergé first decided he would like me better dead.

* * * * *

I had been working for the previous two years for *L'Association des Amis du Congo* (AAC), a non-profit organization that provided humanitarian aid to victims of the Congolese civil war. I made regular trips to East Africa to photograph thirteen year old boys in gun battles and families in squalid refugee camps, and the AAC then published my work in pamphlets and showed my photographs at private exhibitions designed to persuade wealthy French citizens to open their wallets to war victims. This arrangement had been orchestrated by Joseph Danton, Head Curator of the *Musée d'Orsay* in Paris, who was also the Director of the AAC. His family had come to France from the Congo when he was a small child, so he had a special interest in stopping the war there and helping the victims. Danton had personally invited Pierre Bergé to the benefit dinner at the Godenot Gallery that evening: it was my last event with *L'Association des Amis du Congo*, a retrospective of all of my Congo photographs from the previous two years, and Danton had invited only the wealthiest and most influential people he knew. One of the most important among them was Bergé, who had been fashion designer Yves Saint Laurent's lover and business partner for more than fifty years before Saint Laurent's death in 2008.

Bergé had recently announced his decision to auction off the vast collection of art that he and Saint Laurent had collected over the years, with the proceeds going to charity:

the profits were expected to exceed three hundred million euros, and though most of the money was already earmarked for AIDS research, the remainder would amount to tens of millions of euros, and Danton was trying to convince Bergé to spend a little on the Congo—but the evening would not turn out as Danton had hoped.

The Godenot Gallery specialized in modern art, and its airy steel-and-glass pavilion provided an austere setting for my pictures of the lush African jungle. The best of the photographs I had taken for the AAC were hung throughout the gallery's five rooms, and closed-captioned documentary films about the gruesome Congolese wars played on television screens in the corners. A string quartet was playing Haydn in one of the inner rooms, the happy, prancing music a stark counterpoint to the photographic evidence of so much misery.

Danton wended his way through the perfumed and dandied VIPs toward me, carrying two glasses of champagne. He was six feet tall, with a salt-and-pepper afro that was so perfectly trimmed and symmetrical it looked like a helmet, and he had an open, friendly face. He wore a tailored myrtle green suit and a blowzy black tie with a ladybug tie-pin, and the gallery's pinpoint spotlights bobbed in the buffed toes of his black leather shoes. His physical grace made him seem to walk in slow motion.

"Congratulations," he said. "It's already a successful evening." Danton handed me a glass of Perrier-Jouet. "I just got a promise of fifty thousand more euros to run our African logistics next year." We clinked and drank.

In the two years of my contract with the AAC, I had come to respect Danton's shrewdness, sophistication and zeal. He had worked his way out of abject poverty in the slums outside of Paris and into one of the most important positions in the French art world, and he leveraged his influence at the Orsay

Museum to advance his personal philanthropic ambitions. He thought of this as redistributing wealth—he was an avowed anarchist living in a world of privilege, and the contradictions between his personal politics and his elite government position didn't trouble him at all.

"I've never felt at home in these little gatherings," I said to Danton, sipping champagne. "I always feel better with people who *can't* have everything they want."

"Maybe this isn't your natural milieu, Luke," he said, "but you're a natural fundraiser. The fact that you're not impressed earns you respect. The wealthy live to impress but disdain the impressionable."

A hundred or so art patrons, government ministers and board chairmen mingled in the gallery, chit-chatting breezily about my ghastly images. I noticed Pierre Bergé lingering in the Kibati Refugee Camp exhibit, but I thought nothing of it at the time. I had met both Bergé and Yves Saint Laurent many times through my ex-girlfriend Séverine, who was a couture hat designer and had collaborated on some of Saint Laurent's later collections. Since Saint Laurent's death, Bergé rarely appeared at such public gatherings, and now he stared around the room distracted, seeming a little lost, his gaze flitting aimlessly from one photo to the next.

"Your legal obligation to the AAC ends tonight, it's true," said Danton. "But perhaps you'd like to continue working for us all the same. Your work has attracted important attention to our cause."

Danton knew that I had routinely turned down lucrative fashion shoots in the past because the subject bored me, and I wasn't sure how I would feel being tied down to a nonprofit for many years at a time, as generous as the compensation might be. "I don't know," I said. "I feel like I should go back to shooting news for a change, maybe in Tibet or Ukraine."

I noticed the L'Oreal heiress chatting with one of the directors of BNP Paribas about one of my beautifully curated photographs hanging from steel cables nearby: a picture of two boys searching a corpse's pockets, outside the town of Goma. Here were two of France's elite standing in the Godenot Gallery evaluating the merits of a photograph of two of the most forsaken people in Africa, a sight that made my stomach turn. As a journalist, I didn't have moral reservations about my role, but as a fundraiser I felt that I was doing the boys in that photograph a disservice. Through photojournalism, I witnessed suffering as a proxy for the rest of the world, in order to move viewers to look within themselves and consider their own humanity. How they acted once they knew what was going on was their business, but it was important to me that they knew what was going on. As a direct advocate for change with the AAC, however, I was telling people what they should think about what they were witnessing, and that was always dangerous. I sipped my two hundred dollar champagne and looked away.

"I see Giselle is here tonight," Danton said, nodding toward the lobby. "Looking as stunning as ever."

Giselle was whisking a black hooded cape off of her shoulders like a magician conjuring herself out of thin air. She handed the cape to the coat-check girl and flattened the stones of her black agate necklace against her bare chest; the dramatic agates set off her red sleeveless trapeze dress, and her blonde hair fell free to her shoulders, in loose ringlets. Giselle's brow was furled, and when she picked me out of the crowd, standing with Danton in a sea of blue hair and tailored jackets, she ran as fast as her stiletto heels let her across the gallery.

"*Bonsoir*," said Danton. He took Giselle's hand and kissed both her cheeks, which were flushed. "I was just offering Luke a job that I hope you'll convince him to take."

"That sounds wonderful," Giselle said. Her voice was hoarse, as if she had been yelling or crying. "I'm wondering if I could discuss something with Luke in private. Please excuse us." She grabbed my arm and pulled me toward the entrance. I looked an apology at Danton, as I let Giselle tow me to the lobby.

"What is it?!" I said. Giselle led me past the coat-check to the plate glass window looking out onto the Champs-Élysées. Strands of white lights illuminated hoarfrost on the bare branches of the plane trees along the avenue. Giselle pushed me up against the window, which the January air had turned to ice.

"Have you ever heard of Pierre Bergé?" she hissed.

"Of course. He's here tonight!"

"Here?! Why?" She traded positions with me against the window and then ducked down so my body hid her from the crowd inside. "Do you know Jacques Martin, as well?"

"None in particular!" Asking for Jacques Martin in France is like asking for John Smith in America.

"I'm afraid you're about to," Giselle said. "Because a very particular Jacques Martin tracked me down today at your apartment. He wants us to help him steal a painting from Pierre Bergé."

"What!"

"Do you know about the auction at the Grand Palais this weekend? Bergé is selling most of the art he collected with Yves Saint Laurent, and this guy Martin says Bergé owes him a painting."

"So what?" I said. "What does that have to do with us?"

Giselle punched me in the chest with both fists. "Listen for a minute! Martin is holding Benoît hostage, and he says he'll kill him if we don't do what he says."

"Benoît? Hostage?" I finished my champagne and set the

flute on the windowsill. "Giselle, when someone kidnaps one of your friends, that's the detail you lead with. How did Benoît get mixed up in this?"

Benoît was an unemployed City of Paris garbage collector, a friend Giselle and I had met at a hole-in-the-wall neighborhood bar a few blocks from my apartment called the Happy Elephant. The Happy Elephant was the center of my little community in Paris—in fact, I had first met Giselle because she and I were both regulars there, and my old friend Jean-Pierre, the Elephant's owner, had been subsidizing Benoît's bar tab ever since Benoît had lost his job with the city. Despite being unemployed, Benoît still wore his green City of Paris coveralls every day—either as a show of loyalty to the garbage department or because he had no other clothes, we weren't sure. He was a gruff, self-educated philosopher (he had a lot of time on his hands), and he was resourceful and often surprising, but how he could possibly have been taken hostage because of a painting owned by Yves Saint Laurent was beyond me. Yves Saint Laurent had been the flaky top of the upper crust of Parisian society, and Benoît was barely even pie-pan grease.

Giselle said, "Jacques Martin knows Benoît from back in the 1970s. And he used to be Yves Saint Laurent's lover."

"Benoît used to be Yves Saint Laurent's lover?"

"Not Benoît. Martin!"

Giselle reached into her handbag for a folded piece of paper, on which a small, pixillated color picture showed Benoît, dressed in his light green coveralls, bound and gagged on the deck of a river barge. He had one eyebrow raised, as if he couldn't quite believe the indignity he was suffering. In the upper left corner, the sun glinted off of fetid green water, which looked like the Seine.

I turned the paper over. The other side was blank. "When

was this picture taken?"

"I have no idea."

"Jacques Martin gave it to you?"

"Yes. He says he wants the painting as ransom, and if we don't deliver it to him, he'll kill Benoît."

"Let me get this straight," I said. "Someone named Jacques Martin is holding Benoît hostage to force us to steal Yves Saint Laurent's painting from Pierre Bergé? That doesn't even begin to make sense. It's Rube Goldberg."

"Martin says he asked Bergé directly for the painting, but no dice. He wants us either to convince Bergé to give him the painting, or to steal the painting ourselves and give it to him. He says he has a napkin from 1979, on which Yves Saint Laurent wrote a promise to give it to him."

"Why doesn't he just go to court, then?" I wondered if the Napoleonic Legal Code covered table linens. "Do you honestly think Benoît could possibly be connected to Pierre Bergé and Yves Saint Laurent?"

"Well, somebody has to collect their garbage," Giselle said. "Anyway, Jacques Martin is connected to Benoît somehow, and right now Martin's opinion is the only one that matters."

I looked at the picture of Benoît. Benoît loved the Seine, and his dream had always been to captain a barge, to trawl up and down the river waving his hat at people on the banks and talking on the radio to other bargemen, so the irony of his position as hostage on such a barge was pungent. I handed the photo back, and Giselle folded it up and put it back in her purse.

"Why doesn't Martin just buy the painting at this charity auction, if he wants it so much?"

"Apparently, he doesn't have two million euros. It's an important painting by James Ensor, one of Les Vingt."

"What's that? Some kind of art collective?"

"Yes! Les Vingt! The Belgian Expressionist movement! Look, we don't have time for basic art history."

"I agree. We need to call the police!"

"That's not what I meant."

I surveyed the party and noticed Danton motioning for me to come back. It was almost time for his presentation and for my own valedictory speech to the Parisian smart set. I had planned to give a few eyewitness accounts of the terrible plight of Congolese refugees, but now my thoughts were spiraling around my friend Benoît.

"Come on," I said. "Let's see what Monsieur Bergé has to say about this Jacques Martin character." I took her arm and strode purposefully toward the Kibati Refugee exhibit.

"Wait! Luke! You can't just walk up to Pierre Bergé and ask him about his dead lover's lover!"

"What do you suggest, then, if you don't want to go to the police? Isn't that what Martin wanted you to do—contact Bergé about this painting?"

"Martin is a criminal," Giselle said, bewilderingly pointing out the obvious. Just as bewilderingly, she suddenly gave in. "All right, let me handle this."

She readjusted her arm more casually in mine, and we strolled through the gallery more nonchalantly now, greeting our wealthy acquaintances with proper platitudes. Danton joined us for a few strides and confided in a low voice that the guests would be called to dinner in five minutes and that I should meet him in the main hall to officially welcome everyone. I nodded, and Giselle and I continued toward the Kibati hall, where I had seen Bergé a little while before.

The Kibati Refugee Camp was the main gathering place for displaced persons in the state of Nord-Kivu, a region of the Democratic Republic of Congo that bordered Rwanda and Uganda. When I had been there the previous summer, a host of refugees had just arrived fleeing the onslaught of Tutsi warlord Laurent Nkunda, and the French medical charity Médecins Sans Frontières had proclaimed a cholera epidemic. The photographs I had taken at that time, of the ill and war-ravaged refugees, had been hung in a narrow exhibit hall that was paneled in steel and polished to the reflective frost of a mirror, so that, as you walked among the colorful pictures of African refugees, you saw ghostly gray reflections of yourself in-between. We found Pierre Bergé standing alone, transfixed by a portrait of a Hum tribeswoman in a brilliant purple and green kanga. The woman was nursing an infant, which had pearly mucus streaming from its little eyes. The woman's own eyes were haunted, the whites yellow and bloodshot.

"Monsieur Bergé," I said. "I'm delighted to see you again."

Bergé turned and shook my hand with surprising vigor. He was nearly eighty years old, bald except for a friar's ring of white hair, and his belly was pleasantly rotund. He wore a powder blue leisure suit with an extraordinary number of jacket pockets, which made him seem simultaneously like a time traveler from 1973 and a visitor from the future. When the style mavens wear something obviously out of step, every-one marvels and says, "*Comme c'est original!*"

"Do you know my friend Giselle Mounier?" I made a slight bow as I introduced her, and Bergé kissed her hand. Giselle blushed, as was the custom, and Bergé continued to hold her hand, which was not the custom.

"Only by reputation," Bergé said. "I have a friend who bought a Louis XV bedroom suite from you. Comtesse du Boisrouvray? *Enchanté!*" Bergé radiated superiority and gallantry.

"*Egalement*, Monsieur," Giselle said. "I remember her well. How delightful!" She lowered her eyes demurely, fluttered her eyelashes, brought her free hand to her chest and fiddled with her necklace. "My antique shop is a thing of the past now, but I still keep my eyes open for wonderful art and beautiful things, which I know you appreciate."

"There are only two things in life," Bergé said. "Love and beauty." Bergé seemed completely enraptured by Giselle. He still had not released her hand.

"Yes, but beauty is the only one that can be bought," Giselle said, with a knowing little laugh.

"Not if you know where to shop, my dear."

"Speaking of which, I happened to be looking at the Christie's auction list online this morning."

"Yes?" said Bergé.

"They're handling your auction at the Grand Palais, *non*?"

"Yes, yes, of course."

"And I was wondering if you could tell me the story behind your wonderful James Ensor, *The Despair of Pierrot*?"

Bergé blanched. He finally let go of Giselle's hand and took a step back. "How do you know about it?" he yelled. His bald pate reddened, and he took another step back, so that he could extend his entire arm when he pointed an accusatory finger at Giselle. He stood there for a moment, arm outstretched, completely motionless except for his spluttering lips, which could not quite produce the words he wanted. When he finally yelled again, his voice had turned deep and gravelly, welling up from a rockpile of disgust in his gallbladder. "How do you know Jacques Martin?" He looked at me. "What do you have to do with this?"

Bergé's yelling had attracted the attention of everyone in the Kibati hall: champagne flutes stopped halfway to heavily painted lips, eyes widened, massive diamonds groaned scornfully in their settings. It was a stationary riot. Heavy footsteps came pounding up the hall, echoing off of the polished steel walls so it sounded as if a small army of Dantons was coming; and as Danton arrived, Bergé reached into his coat pocket and withdrew a six inch long titanium rod. He held it up, like a rapier, then removed its cap to reveal a silver fountain pen. He showed it to us, nodding a toothy grin like a silent film villain, then whirled suddenly and plunged the pen into the photograph he had just been admiring, of the Hum tribeswoman nursing her baby. The pen stabbed into the folds of the woman's sleeve, through the pressed-foam mounting board, and quivered there like an arrow.

"Pierre!" Danton cried. He rushed up and took Bergé's arm. "What's wrong, Pierre?"

Bergé pointed his accusing finger at me and Giselle. "Ask them!" He yanked his arm out of Danton's grip and stormed down the hall toward the main pavilion. Danton followed right on his heels, pleading with him to calm down and tell him what was the matter.

Thirty or so of the richest and most influential citizens of Paris encircled me and Giselle in a loose ring, sipping from their cut-crystal champagne flutes menacingly. A cold wave of social horror slapped against us, like the surge of a tide that brings a dead body ashore, and even the string quartet in the back room stopped playing. Only the echoes of Danton's increasingly distant, frantic pleas broke the silence.

Giselle had turned as white as marble. I put my hand on her back.

"This is going to be bad for donations," I said.

2

The Mysterious Jacques Martin

Danton remained away from the party for nearly five minutes—an insult to the rest of his guests, who could only surmise that they were not as important as Pierre Bergé. They angrily demanded explanations of Giselle and me, and when we protested that we didn't understand what had happened, the crowd snubbed us, en masse, simply turned their backs and refused to look at us, which felt surprisingly horrible. Giselle cried, and when Danton returned, the grim look on his face caused her to run out of the gallery. I tried to stop her, but she slapped my hand away, and Danton hooked his index finger at me and turned toward the rear of the gallery. I was caught between my girlfriend and my employer, and I unchivalrously chose Danton.

As Danton excused us and we left the hall for a back office, the urbane crowd erupted in newly outraged chatter, which sounded like the chimpanzee squawks one hears from the trees in the Congo. The string quartet played "The Chicken Reel," which I thought an extraordinarily cheeky and obscure commentary coming from Parisian chamber musicians.

Danton yelled at me, to no avail. I understood little more about what had just happened than he did, and when I explained what I did know, we were both equally in the dark. Danton had never heard of Jacques Martin, either.

"Well, there's nothing we can do about it right now," he finally said. "Let's see if we can save the dinner." He composed himself and adjusted his tie, and we returned to the party.

The crowd, which had nearly mingled itself into unconsciousness before, was now electric with scandal, and they hung on every word Danton said. He made some rather generic remarks of apology, which did not win the crowd back; but then he channeled all of his mortification and embarrassment into an impassioned appeal for the Congo. He spoke with increasing fervor and eloquence, ending with a truly horrific account of the epidemics sweeping the refugee camps.

When he had finished speaking, the crowd applauded politely, and Danton led everyone into the anterior gallery, where the banquet tables were set with red linens and white ceramic swans. He did not even bother introducing me but instead shooed me off to my seat. At his signal, the string quartet returned to playing traditional chamber ditties, and Danton trotted around to each table to offer his personal apologies, while tuxedo-clad waiters served *poularde de bresse aux morilles*. By the time the apricot clafoutis arrived for dessert, the guests had become almost amenable again, and the AAC ended the eventful evening with three hundred thousand euros in new pledges. However, three hundred thousand was small potatoes next to the tens of millions Pierre Bergé had stormed out with. When I left after dinner, Danton shook my hand coldly, without looking me in the eye.

* * * * *

Giselle and I spent a restless night at my apartment, in the Marais. The Marais is a complex, culturally mixed neighborhood that straddles the third and fourth arrondissements. Originally a swamp, the area was drained in the twelfth century by the Knights Templar, who allowed various religious orders to maintain vegetable gardens there for the next two hundred years. In the fourteenth century, aristocrats began building grand mansions in the Marais—a development that culminated in the early 1600s, when Henri IV constructed the Place des Vosges in the center of the *quartier* and made it the seat of the royal court. When Louis XIV decided to move his court and government to Versailles in 1682 and the royals followed him out of town, the stone palaces of the Marais fell into neglect. The neighborhood was so run down by the time Baron Hausmann began his architectural reinvention of Paris in the 1860s that Hausmann avoided it almost altogether, directing his grand boulevards toward other areas of the city and leaving the slums of the Marais in squalor and dilapidation. The area became a landing point for penniless immigrants, Jews and other ethnic minorities first coming to Paris, and in the Second World War it harbored refugees. Even through the 1960s, the term Marais was synonymous with ghetto; but then, unexpectedly, beginning in the 1980s, real estate developers discovered the charm of the ancient structures and began refurbishing them. By the time I moved there in the late 1990s, the Marais had become one of the most attractive *quartiers* in Paris. The Place des Vosges had been restored to magnificent apartments surrounding an open square with burbling fountains and garden paths—a place where families congregated for play dates, lovers met for romantic walks and film societies screened classic New Wave films under the open night sky; and the Marais remained a vital center for Orthodox Jews. On my block, synagogues stood next to trendy cafes, and African Muslims sold fresh produce from tiny vegetable stands.

I had moved into this neighborhood when I'd needed a European home base while working for the New York *Times*. My apartment, on rue des Tournelles, was quite typical of Paris. A fifth-floor walk-up, it had an eighty square foot main room that contained my bed, a desk and two chairs. Next to the main room was a narrow kitchen with a tiny refrigerator and a two-burner hotplate; and beyond the kitchen, the cramped bathroom shared a wall and most of its pipes with the kitchen. As a small measure of luxury, windows in each room looked out onto a pleasant inner courtyard.

Giselle and I sat staring into the courtyard. Now, in the dead of winter, the dim gray moonlight made the empty flowerboxes across the way seem like dark bags below the eyes of the neighbor's windows. Giselle held a glass of armagnac in one hand and the photograph of Benoît, gagged and bound on a barge, in the other. Her legs were folded underneath her in the chair opposite mine.

"We have to go to the police," I said.

"If we go to the police and Benoît gets hurt or killed because of it, I'll never forgive myself."

"How about if we don't go to the police, and Benoît gets hurt or killed, will you forgive yourself then? We can't help Benoît on our own—we don't even know where he is—and we can't commit grand larceny against Pierre Bergé just hoping it all works out."

"It does seem rather hopeless to try to steal a painting from the Grand Palais, doesn't it?"

"Impossible! It might as well be a fortress."

All of Bergé's art for the auction had already been moved to the Grand Palais, near Pont Alexandre III, where the sale would take place. Every major Parisian newspaper had splashed color photos of the most valuable paintings and sculptures across their pages during the past week—anything connected to Yves Saint Laurent still commanded attention in Paris, especially when it was worth half a billion dollars.

"But Martin told me specifically not to go to the police, or it was curtains for Benoît!"

Giselle finished her armagnac and reached for the bottle on the table between us. She poured us each another drink.

"Giselle, we don't even know if Martin's story is true!"

"Some part of it must be true. Otherwise, why would Bergé have reacted so violently? I didn't even mention Martin's name: I asked about the painting, *The Despair of Pierrot*, and Bergé immediately said 'Jacques Martin' and flew into a rage."

"That's true. How did you leave it with Martin?"

"I gave him my cell number," she said. "He said he'd call with further instructions."

Giselle described her encounter with Martin, here at my apartment, the previous day. He had buzzed the intercom from the street and identified himself as a client from Giselle's old antique shop.

"I should never have buzzed him in," Giselle said. "I mean, why would he know to look for me at *your* apartment in the first place, if he was just a former client? But he said he had a question about a Directoire vase that I had bought at an estate sale five years ago and sold to a friend of his—I actually remembered the vase, and his friend! Somehow, he knows things about the history of my shop, or at least about that estate sale, so I let my guard down."

"He would have found a way to get to us one way or another. He wouldn't have kidnapped Benoît without knowing how he was going to use him."

Giselle shook her head in a dreamy, rueful way. "He seemed harmless when he came to the door." She said Martin was a mushroom of a man, short and stout with a bulbous, bald head too big for his body. She guessed he was in his mid-seventies, and his skin was leathered and full of brown splotches. He had been perfectly polite, even while threatening Giselle with ransom demands. "He was businesslike, as if he really were inquiring about a Directoire vase," she said. "He even asked for a cup of tea." Before she knew what had happened, the little old mushroom was gone, leaving behind Benoît's photo and a promise to contact her again. "I was still sort of in shock when I arrived at the gallery. It's hard to believe it really happened."

"None of this persuades me not to go to the police," I said. I sipped my armagnac and was thinking I could just go to the police by myself and tell them everything I knew, with or without Giselle's approval, when a low rumbling echoed through the stairwell.

Residents of my building come and go at all hours, so footsteps on the stairs usually don't alarm me, but there was something about the leaden stomping now that gave me pause. The steps pounded closer and closer, until they stopped on my own landing. Low voices spoke. The floorboards creaked. My doorbell rang.

"Did you give Martin the building codes?" I asked. Two doors, with two separately coded electronic locks, blocked the way from the street to the inner courtyard. Giselle shook her head no. Whoever was outside my apartment—at three in the morning!—either had to know both codes or figure out how to bypass them.

I quietly rose from my chair and tip-toed across the room. Just as I put my eye to the peephole, a fist banged the door, and my heart pinballed into my throat. "Open up! Police!" To calm myself, I slowly counted the number of years I had just lost off the end of my life. I was up to five when the voice shouted again. Through the fish-eye lens in my door, I could see the blue-jacketed arm of a Police Nationale uniform.

"Looks like we won't have to go to the police, after all."

I opened the door. A strapping young policeman stood at my threshold, next to my building's sixty-year-old concierge, in a threadbare pink bathrobe and bunny-rabbit slippers. She seemed to be mentally reviewing my residency agreement for ways of throwing me out. Behind her, three more policemen stood at the ready.

The officer at the door looked right past me. "Giselle Mounier?"

"Oui." Giselle stood up.

"Doesn't anyone look for you at your own apartment any more?" I said to her.

"In fact, Monsieur, we are searching her apartment right now," the officer said. "You are Luke Johnson?"

"That's right."

"You'll come with us, too."

"Too?"

"I'm here to arrest Madame Mounier on charges of illegal entry and larceny. We will also have to search this apartment." The concierge's bunny-rabbit slippers smiled up at me.

"Larceny?" I said. "For stealing what?"

"We have reason to believe that she stole a painting from the Grand Palais."

Giselle sucked a deep breath through her teeth. She lifted both hands to show the policemen they were empty, then tilted her head to the side, indicating her half-full glass of armagnac. The officer nodded obligingly, and Giselle picked up her drink and drained it.

"This painting wouldn't happen to be *The Despair of Pierrot*, would it?" I asked.

The officer narrowed his eyes and waved the other policemen into my apartment. Giselle and I put on our coats while they began their search, bumping and stumbling around each other in the tiny space like Keystone Kops.

The officer in charge took Giselle by the arm and led her out to the landing, where we were both frisked and handcuffed. We descended the stairs awkwardly, Giselle in front with her escort, me following with my own policeman. Three more bluecoats were waiting for us at ground level, and they led us to two idling squad cars that were blocking the street. A small crowd had gathered to witness the fuss. The policemen helped Giselle into the back seat of the first car, and she looked at me through the window, wild-eyed.

"Tell them everything you know," I yelled. "I'll call Jean-Pierre and Danton, you call Manon and your lawyer."

Giselle did not seem comforted by this list of allies. Her car sped off and disappeared around the corner onto rue de Rivoli, and I was stuffed ignominiously into the back of the second car.

3

SÉVERINE'S HAT SHOP

After several hours of questioning, the police released me from the Les Halles Station. I had told them all I knew, especially pleading with them to pursue Benoît's captor, Jacques Martin; and though they shared my opinion that Martin's ransom demand was both mystifying and unbelievable, they assumed that was because I was making the whole story up. They continued to hold Giselle, though they had no more evidence against her than they had against me—I figured that they probably just wanted me to lead them to the painting and held onto her as insurance that I wouldn't flee.

I felt very alone as I walked along the rue aux Ours away from the police station. The morning sun spread light the color of nonfat margarine across the grimy seventeenth century stone apartments. It was just after nine o'clock. To the prim, well-shaved people I met on the street, it was just another work day, and I looked like I'd had a little too much fun the night before. I took out my cell phone and started to dial Jean-Pierre at the Happy Elephant, but I wondered if it would transmit everything I said directly to the police, now that I was under surveillance. The GPS monitoring system would certainly upload my every movement into their database. I turned the phone off.

* * * * *

When I got back to my apartment, I discovered that the

cops had done a discreet job of searching, replacing nearly everything exactly the way they had found it except for a box of Petit Beurre biscuits. The biscuit box had been unopened before but now sat half-empty on the kitchen counter. I bit into one, found that it had gone stale overnight and decided to go down to the Happy Elephant, to see Jean-Pierre in person, have an espresso and figure out what to do next.

L'Elephant Heureux was the wine bar Jean-Pierre had dreamed of opening for more then twenty years, while he drudged away in his first career as a board operator at Radio France. He had finally managed to finance the place ten years before and, in the time since, had become more and more like a happy elephant himself, appearing slower, bulkier and more content with each passing year. His long, curly, gray beard and sparkling brown eyes gave him a jolly philosophical air.

I had known Jean-Pierre since I was in my early twenties and just starting out as a photojournalist, and it was our friendship from his days at Radio France that had originally made me a regular at the Happy Elephant. Jean-Pierre could always be counted on to listen sympathetically and stroke his beard with Aristotelian gravity while his customers drunkenly explained their latest theories of life. His clientele reflected his own sensibility, in being cosmopolitan and ambitious but laissez-faire about everyday events.

When I arrived at the Happy Elephant this morning, I found Jean-Pierre outside sweeping the sidewalk. He never opened the bar before five in the evening, but he liked to fill his entire day with menial, preparatory tasks. The bar was small, a one-man operation with only ten stools and half a dozen tables, so there was never much to do, but Jean-Pierre found that if he did each task slowly enough, it almost amounted to a full-time job and gave him plenty of time to chat with his friends, who were constantly dropping by.

"*Salut*, Luke," he said. He gave my shoulder a friendly pat and then whistled gravely. "I hope you don't feel as bad as you look."

"Worse."

Jean-Pierre ushered me inside and went behind the bar to fix us each an espresso, while I told him everything that had happened. "I saw a story about the theft on television this morning," Jean-Pierre said. "The thieves didn't even trip the alarm, and the videos from the security cameras show nothing. One second the painting is there, the next second it's gone. Poof."

"It's especially bad timing, too," he added. "The Grand Palais was hosting a public showing of all the pieces this week, before the auction. The gallery had even re-created some of the bedrooms from Yves Saint Laurent's house, so they could display the art the way it had been hung in his home. It looks bad for everyone: Christie's, the police, the RMN." RMN stands for *Réunion des Musées Nationaux*, the arm of the French Ministry of Culture that runs the museums. "I'm surprised you're not still in custody."

"They don't have any clues," I said, "so they want me to lead them to some."

"And Benoît?"

"I don't know. Either Martin has the painting now or someone else does, so there's no point in his threatening to kill Benoît."

"Unless Martin thinks *you* have the painting."

Jean-Pierre poured our coffees and set them on the bar. I sat down, sipped my espresso and felt the weariness behind my eyes grow thinner and more taut with the caffeine.

"That's a good point. We think Martin has the painting, Martin thinks we have the painting. Benoît is in the middle. But who does have the painting?"

I finished my coffee and stared out at the street. The water valves on rue des Tournelles had opened, and two City of Paris street sweepers, wearing light green jumpsuits, were directing the flow of water down the gutters with filthy brooms. This ritual, performed twice daily in central Paris, became more hypnotic the more times I saw it, especially after sleepless nights.

"I think I need to talk to Pierre Bergé," I said. "He's the only one who seems to know who Jacques Martin is. And he must be the one who turned us in for stealing the painting in the first place."

"How do you know?"

"Who else could it have been? He freaks out last night when Giselle mentions the painting, immediately accuses us of being in Martin's camp, then he goes home, learns that the painting is missing and tells the cops about our encounter at the Godenot Gallery. What else could have brought the cops to my door so quickly?"

Jean-Pierre stroked his beard. "If you get within ten meters of Bergé, the cops will break you in half."

"Obviously, I can't just walk up to him, and I doubt Danton can get to him, either, after the fiasco last night."

Jean-Pierre fixed me a look. "Séverine, then."

"Séverine," I agreed.

I had dated Séverine for eight years. In fact, Séverine and I had still been dating when Giselle and I had first slept together, and the fact that Séverine and Giselle had been friends for many years before that made the betrayal all the more bitter. In the two years since our break-up, Séverine and I had reached détente—after all, her hat shop was just around the corner from my apartment, so we saw each other frequently on the street, and she was still friends with Jean-Pierre and Benoît—but we were merely cordial, even now, and Séverine still despised Giselle. But Séverine had worked with Yves Saint Laurent for many years, and she would have no trouble at all getting a meeting with Bergé. Even if Séverine wouldn't jump at the chance to come to Giselle's rescue, her feelings for Benoît would persuade her to help.

"Call Séverine, will you?" I asked Jean-Pierre. "Tell her I'll come to her shop."

Jean-Pierre picked up the phone and dialed, and I went behind the bar to make myself another espresso. From listening only to Jean-Pierre's end of the conversation, it quickly became apparent that Séverine already knew about the painting and our unfortunate confrontation with Bergé at the AAC fundraiser. Jean-Pierre hung up and raised his eyebrows at me.

"Bergé is on his way to Séverine's shop right now. She says he's been trying to reach you."

"Bergé's trying to reach me?" I made us each another espresso and sat down again at the bar.

"It makes sense," Jean-Pierre said. "The police have Giselle. Benoît is tied up somewhere, the painting is missing, and this Jacques Martin is on the loose. You and Bergé have to help each other."

* * * * *

Séverine's hat shop was on rue des Francs-Bourgeois, one of the trendiest streets in the Marais, and therefore in all of Paris, within a stone's throw of the Carnavalet's *jardin à la française*. Three other couture hat shops thrived within walking distance of Séverine's, an indication of how seriously the French take their heads.

As I walked briskly through the Place des Vosges, huddled into my gray peacoat, I searched the avenue for undercover police. Any one of a dozen people might have been follow-ing me. I turned my phone on and dialed Giselle, and a deep baritone voice answered, "This is Officer Nadeau. Madame Mounier can't speak now. Is this Luke Johnson?"

"Doesn't it say so on the digital display?"

"It does. Madame Mounier wants you to bring her an overnight bag and a change of clothes. She's probably going to be here for quite some time."

"On what grounds?"

The line went dead. I turned off the phone again.

When I arrived at *Chapellerie Séverine*, Pierre Bergé was already there. I saw him through the picture window, gesticulating wildly at Séverine, wearing the same powder blue leisure suit he had worn at the Godenot Gallery the night before, but now he topped it with a ladies' pink angora cloche hat. In fact, he and Séverine were wearing identical pink angora cloches, which made their heated discussion seem cartoonish. I walked in, and Bergé stopped speaking in mid-sentence. He reached for the hat, I assumed in embarrassment, but instead of taking it off, he adjusted it forward so that it covered more of his brow. Séverine removed hers, freeing her gleaming black curls, and set the hat on a metal disc on the glass display counter at her elbow.

Séverine's haute couture collaborators often gave her samples of their latest designs, so she was always six months ahead of the trends. Today, she wore a form-fitting cerise satin wrap, with an emerald green jacket over it and matching green stockings.

"I don't understand you, Luke," Séverine said, by way of a greeting.

I interpreted this remark to mean, "See? You left me for that bitch Giselle, who is nothing but a trouble-maker and criminal and now, because of her, you're mixed up in a national embarrassment and you may get our friend Benoît killed and yourself in the bargain, if you're not merely jailed for the rest of your life! All the while you could have been married to me and making a fabulous living as a fashion photographer, and we would actually be happy! Or doesn't happiness appeal to you? What a fool you are, and what a fool I was to have loved you for so long, and now you have the audacity to involve me, through my friend Pierre Bergé, in something disreputable, something that will probably rob me of the last sliver of good will I have toward humanity. You are turning me into a bitter woman, and you ruin everything you touch. How can life be so unsatisfactory?"

"Hello," I said.

"I suppose you have no idea where Jacques Martin is?" Bergé said.

"I have no idea *who* Jacques Martin is!"

"Martin is a charlatan, a liar and a thief."

"A kidnapper, too," I added. "But I've never met the man, and I have no idea where he is. Did you tell the police I stole your painting?"

"Didn't you?!" Bergé spat.

"That's not an answer."

"Yes, I told them you stole my painting. You and Jacques Martin and that blonde you're with."

"I had nothing to do with it," I said. "I'd never even heard of it till yesterday, or of James Ensor, for that matter."

"What!" Bergé yelled. Not knowing James Ensor seemed an even worse offense in his book than stealing one of Ensor's paintings. He actually growled a little. "James Ensor was one of the most important Expressionists in Belgium!"

To me, this was as meaningful as shouting, "Pensacola is the Monte Carlo of Florida!"

"Ensor used burlesque figures to comment on modern

life," Bergé continued. "And he transformed ancient religious themes into scathing political commentaries." Bergé pounded his fist on the glass display case. "Without Ensor, there is no Egon Schiele or Alvar Cawen or Wassily Kandinsky. He painted the very soul of modern man and nearly frightened Belgium out of the First World War!"

This litany seemed ridiculous in light of the pink angora hat Bergé was wearing. "That's all very well," I said, "but why don't we concentrate on the most important aspect of James Ensor, which is: who has your painting? I'm betting Jacques Martin does."

"Martin!" Bergé pulled the cloche down tight around his ears.

Séverine looked at the hat in alarm, calculating the number of rabbits that had been sheared to make it. "Could you please calm down and tell each other what you know?" Séverine said. "There's more at stake here than a painting." She turned to me. "You really have no idea who Jacques Martin is?"

Every time anyone mentioned the name Jacques Martin, Pierre Bergé involuntarily stomped and spat. "I swear I don't," I said, "but from the first time I heard his name, bad things have been happening." By this time, I thought, Martin had probably sold the painting to the Hong Kong mafia. "Could you please tell me who this person is, and maybe we can figure this out?"

All of the wind seemed suddenly to go out of Bergé's sails, and he leaned heavily against the display case he had just been abusing. He asked Séverine for a glass of water. She reached underneath the cash register and, in a few short moments, produced a tray holding a bottle of Perrier, a chilled glass with a lemon slice already in it and a plate of chocolate shortbreads. She was used to entertaining finicky, wealthy clients, and she kept a small icebox stocked with treats.

We waited while Bergé refreshed himself. Séverine

pointedly refused to meet my eyes. It had been long enough, I thought, for both of us to have recovered emotionally and moved on to other relationships, and we should long ago have patched up our friendship; but Séverine was not so magnanimously disposed, and she was the injured party in the break-up, so it was not my place to tell her how forgiving she should be. It seemed that her new boyfriend might have eased her pain a little, but she clung to her scorn.

Bergé snacked as if he were taking afternoon tea at the George V, apparently feeling no need even to make small talk, so the interlude seemed to stretch for an hour. Finally, Bergé washed down his chocolates with the last of the Perrier, stretched his arms and stood up, ready to condescend again.

"I first heard of Jacques Martin two weeks ago," Bergé said. "An envelope was delivered by messenger to my apartment. The envelope contained a letter and a photograph of a napkin. On the napkin was a nearly indecipherable scrawl that Martin claimed was Yves' promise to give him *The Despair of Pierrot* whenever Yves died."

The letter Bergé had received claimed that Jacques Martin and Yves Saint Laurent had been secret lovers from 1968 to 1980, and that they had renewed their affair just a few months before Saint Laurent had died in 2008. In the letter, Martin gave many corroborating details, of specific places and dates when he and Saint Laurent had been together, many of which aligned with times when Bergé had been away from Paris. "However," Bergé said. "Any clever person could have tracked Yves' movements at that time, just by reading the press. Yves was a public figure, known all over the world, and it's not evidence of your involvement with a celebrity to know where he is on a certain date."

Martin had claimed that *The Despair of Pierrot* was a special token of the bond that existed between him and Saint

Laurent, that he had convinced Saint Laurent to buy it and that the painting had even hung for more than a year in Martin's own apartment, in the late nineteen-seventies. "I will admit," Bergé said, "that Yves and I were sometimes estranged, and that we had many residences, so I would not necessarily have known where any one painting was at any one time. I admit it, but that proves nothing."

Séverine cleared her throat. "Not to be indiscreet, Pierre, but had you remained lovers with Yves all that time? I thought you two had split up romantically long ago."

Bergé exploded. "We were married in a civil union just days before he died!"

Séverine remained unruffled. "But Pierre, you introduced me to several of your other lovers while Yves and I were working together over the years. Yves had other lovers, as well. It was no great secret!"

Bergé wilted back onto the stool and selected another chocolate shortbread from the tray. Séverine turned to me with a look of doubt and complicity, as if she were now allowing me to switch sides, to form an alliance with her so that we could manage Pierre. "Pierre and Yves were business partners for fifty years," she told me. "You know how successful they made each other, how well they worked together, but they had a falling out decades ago that affected the rest of their relationship. Isn't that right, Pierre?"

I had never seen anyone over the age of eight look as melodramatically glum as Pierre Bergé did then. "Yes, we split more than thirty years ago. We would be with each other occasionally after that, sometimes for a few months, sometimes just for a few days, but never for long. Never like it was in the old days. But it is a fact that Yves and I were married just before his death, and he left his entire estate to me. That is a fact." He threw his hands up as if he were about to yell again, but his spirit collapsed on itself. "Yves loved me."

Séverine breathed in deeply through her nose, widening her eyes meaningfully, as if to say that Bergé's fragility was our biggest problem. The self-righteousness had left her eyes, and I wondered if she would think badly of me if, at that moment, I ate a chocolate shortbread. I hadn't eaten since dinner the night before.

I said to Bergé, "Why would it have been impossible for Martin to have a relationship with Yves?"

"*The Despair of Pierrot* was our painting," Bergé said. "Yves and I loved that painting. It's the whole reason we started collecting Expressionists." He was on the verge of weeping. "It's a symbol of the love that Yves and I shared. We spent many nights talking about romance and lust, brotherhood and sex. That painting encapsulated the philosophy of our longing, the cruelty and splendor of needing another person so intimately, with all your heart, in your body, in your mind, that you will do anything for him. It was the external projection of us and even contains an intimation of Christ as a clown, the idea that the highest love possible is mocked in this world. The idea that that same painting could be a special token between Yves and me and Yves and this fool Martin is a complete lie. Yves would not betray me in this way."

That was a lot of weight to put on a painting, I thought, but now I could see, at least, what was at stake. It was not money or crime or even art but love. Perhaps Saint Laurent had renewed all of his love affairs at the end of his life, as a way of reconciling himself to death, even at the very moment that he had entered into a civil union with Bergé, an idea that could only infuriate Bergé.

"Weren't you about to sell that painting at auction?" I said. "If it has such sentimental value for you, why were you selling it?"

"How I deal with my feelings is nobody's affair but my own," Bergé said. "*The Despair of Pierrot* has sentimental value for me and Yves, not Martin and Yves, and Martin had no right to steal it just because of his nostalgia. If I want to sell it, fine. I own it. If Martin wants to steal it, that just makes him a common thief."

"So you do think Martin stole it?"

"I think no one could steal a painting from the National Gallery of the Grand Palais without the help of sophisticated accomplices." He looked at me accusingly.

"I've already told you half a dozen times, I had nothing to do with it."

"Then it's Martin!" he thundered.

It still made no sense: you don't hold someone hostage as ransom bait for a painting you're going to steal yourself. Someone besides Martin had to be involved somehow. "In the letter you received from him demanding the painting, how were you supposed to deliver it?"

"He demanded that I allow a representative of his to pick the painting up from me at Yves' home. Of course, by that time, it was already in the Grand Palais."

"And no extra precautions were taken to secure the painting?" Séverine said. "You get a disturbing note demanding a painting and yet you allow that very painting to be stolen?"

"I allowed nothing!" Bergé said. "In the first place, my dear Séverine, the Grand Palais is fairly well guarded, I think you'll agree. And in the second place, by the time I contacted the RMN to alert them of the demand, the painting had already disappeared."

I touched Séverine's arm. "May I speak to you privately for a moment?"

Séverine recoiled a bit at my touch, but she conceded. "Will you excuse us, Pierre?" she said.

Bergé nodded disconsolately and asked if there were any almond shortbread cookies, and Séverine promised to bring him some. She led me through a door at the back of her boutique, to her atelier, a cramped, white-plastered room that was a riot of adjustable drafting surfaces, cutting tables, fabrics, styrofoam heads, measuring tapes, protractors and binding plasters.

"Can Bergé be trusted?" I whispered.

"As much as you can," she said ironically.

"What did he tell you before I got here?"

She put her hand to the back of her neck, massaged the muscles at the base of her skull and grimaced. Though I am not usually a fan of perfume, the designer scent she wore this morning was working its well-formulated magic, some Berber musk blended with hot sand and honey that reminded me of a Moroccan seashore.

"How do you get into these situations, Luke?"

"I didn't get into anything. You have to believe me! The only reason I'm here at all is Benoît."

She closed her eyes and thought for a moment. Her eye shadow was exactly the same shade of cerise as her dress. "He was asking me about Benoît. A lot of strange questions."

"Like what?"

"He wanted to know if Benoît was gay, for one thing. He wanted to know if he had ever gone by the name Napoleon le Tigre."

"You're kidding!"

"I have no idea how he even knew that I knew Benoît. I thought he called me this morning because he knew that I knew you, but he seems determined to find out about Benoît."

"Is Benoît gay?"

"I doubt it. I mean, I've never heard him talk about loving anyone, come to think of it, man or woman. All he ever talks about is the Seine. What's it called when you have a sexual preference for a river?"

I almost laughed. Séverine never joked about anything, and now she was cracking wise when Benoît's life might be on the line. She moved in closer to me, until I could feel her breath when she whispered.

"What do you think is happening, Luke?" She brought her hand to my cheek and caressed my jaw and neck.

"I don't know," I said, though now I was talking about what she was doing. She kissed me on the lips, a full gentle kiss that was inappropriate for so many reasons it would require an Expressionist painting to depict them all.

"I've missed you, Luke," she whispered, and then she kissed me again, and I let her. And then I was kissing her!

"Wait. What are you doing?"

"What are you doing?"

"What?"

"What?!"

I nodded over her shoulder toward Bergé, who was coming across the showroom toward the atelier. Séverine ran her hands down her dress and looked at the floor for a moment, and by the time she looked up again, her eyes had filled with tears.

We met Bergé together. "Have you been kissing?" he shouted. "How can you be kissing at a time like this? Have you no respect for the dead?"

"The dead?" I could understand why Bergé would be offended, but I wasn't sure what our kissing had to do with Yves Saint Laurent. If anything, our disrespect had fallen entirely on Bergé. Or Benoît.

Bergé snatched the pink rabbit cloche from his head and threw it to the floor. Then he stormed out of Séverine's boutique, swearing loudly about how I was an art thief and he would not allow us make a fool out of him. Apparently, Bergé was in the habit of storming out of buildings. Séverine rushed out the door after him.

I was still no closer to Benoît, Jacques Martin or *The Despair of Pierrot* than before. And I had just kissed my ex-girlfriend, who had cried, while my current girlfriend was in jail. So far, it had not been my best day.

4

Secrets

When Séverine came back into her shop, her cheeks were flushed. "Why did you kiss me?"

"Why did *you* kiss *me*?"

"That's no answer!"

In truth, there are few enough reasons why people kiss each other, and fewer still that require explanation. "You started it!"

"Well, a kiss can sometimes be the most direct way to communicate the most convoluted kinds of information," she said.

"Information? You mean feelings!"

"You're so American sometimes."

"What does that have to do with anything?"

She threw up her arms. "It's complicated," she said.

In French culture, the best way of buying time or getting off the hook entirely in a thorny personal situation is to claim that it's complicated. The French did not invent love, but they did invent romance, so they've had more time than any other culture on earth to refine the nuances of its language. What to Americans are straightforward and easily defined cases of sin or virtue can become, to the French, almost inexplicable abstractions, mazes of emotion where lovers can lose themselves and each other. In a French love affair, grandeur is better than clarity, so claiming that things are complicated and gesturing in a way that demonstrates deep thought gains you instant credibility. If you're French, that is.

"It's not complicated at all," I said. She took a step toward me. "What are you doing?"

"I'm going to kiss you, and you're going to let me. You're going to kiss me, too."

"I am?"

"Yes."

"Why am I?"

"Because you want to."

I became aware that window shoppers on rue des Franc-Bourgeois were peering in at us. Séverine put her hands on my hips. She kissed me. I did not kiss her back, but I did not stop her, a compromise that satisfied no one. I stepped away and knelt to pick up the pink angora cloche that Pierre Bergé had flung away so violently. I handed it to Séverine, unconsciously placing all of my hopes for resolution in the rabbit-wool hat. She took it and worked it back into its proper bell shape.

"Try it on," Séverine said. She held the hat out to me.

"It's a woman's hat."

She walked to the counter and got its twin, the hat she had been wearing when I first came in. She slipped her hat on and pushed the other one out to me again. I put the pink hat on. The window shoppers outside were now staring with real interest.

She kissed me again, and now we were two ex-lovers in pink cloche hats kissing as a window display! Somehow, even in this bizarre scenario, Séverine's thick lips felt good enveloping my own, and I reached up to touch a ringlet of her hair hanging in front of her ear, which was when I realized that I had completely lost my mind.

"Séverine!"

"All right," she said. "What are we going to do about Benoît, then?"

"We?"

She put a hand on my chest. "He's my friend, too," she said. "Don't you have a boyfriend?"

"Yes, of course," she breathed at me. "What does he have to do with it?"

I took off the hat and set it on the counter. This bored the shoppers on the street, who flounced off toward merrier destinations.

"Okay, then," I said, "what are we going to do about Benoît?"

Séverine pursed her lips in a look of pure fury. Apparently, it was perfectly acceptable for her to ask what we were going to do about Benoît, but I was not allowed. She turned on one heel and ran gawkily into her atelier.

"Séverine!" I called.

I looked around the boutique, at all of the absurdly elaborate bonnets, caps and trilbys that Séverine had made by hand. Outside, the day was turning dark and gray, and the air, even inside the shop, was brittle with approaching snow. Séverine was rummaging noisily in the workshop.

What *were* we going to do about Benoît? I thought. He was obviously our only connection to Martin, and now that the police were holding Giselle, and Giselle's cell phone, Martin had no way to contact me directly, even presuming he wanted to. It was possible that he already had the painting, so there might be no reason for him to contact us ever again. On the contrary, it seemed that we would now be obliged to find him in order to clear our names with the police, and there was still the possibility that he would hurt Benoît, whether he had the painting or not.

I entered Séverine's workshop. At first, I didn't even see her, sitting on a low spinning stool in the far back corner, hidden by a mound of fabrics on a table, her face to the wall.

"Séverine?"

She snuffled. "I've missed you, Luke. Everyone says you're a jerk and I should forget about you, but I still can't believe you left me for Giselle. I don't understand why that happened." She spun around. "Were you that unhappy with me?"

"No, Séverine." I knelt so that we were at eye level. I took both of her hands in mine.

"You just need change, don't you? You need adventure. But I thought you got that from your work. I thought you got enough excitement from those godforsaken wars in the Middle East, in Africa, wherever. I thought Paris would be a quiet home for us. That we could have a calm, happy life together here. Now you make as much trouble for yourself here as you have everywhere else in the world." She wiped her eyes with the backs of her hands. "I can't believe this is the life you really want."

"I don't want trouble," I said. "I didn't become a war photographer because I like trouble, I became a war photographer so people would know about the problems in the world, about the things that people do to each other."

"So why couldn't you make a quiet life with me here in Paris? What was wrong with our life?"

"Nothing. We had a wonderful life together."

She ran her index finger down the length of my nose. I thought of Pierre Bergé and Jacques Martin and Yves Saint Laurent, the trouble that that love triangle was causing now, even after Yves Saint Laurent had died. In love, three's a crowd: at least the Americans got that one right.

Séverine kissed the tip of my nose. "You should go take care of Giselle," she said sadly.

The crash of breaking glass exploded through Séverine's boutique. We jumped up and ran to the showroom, where we found the brick that had come bursting through a plate glass window. It had tumbled to a stop in the middle of the room, amid a fantastic spray of shards and splinters. A note was tied to it with twine.

Séverine unfolded the note and read a message scrawled across the page in charcoal. "Les Frigos, *de minuit ce soir.*" She held the note out to me. "They ruined my window for this?!"

I was shocked, as well. People still used bricks to deliver messages? Had the nineteenth century never left the Marais? After all, the door to the shop was unlocked, and Séverine's phone number and email address were printed right there on the glass they had broken.

A cold wind blew through the hole in the window, ruffling the ostrich feathers of a purple Tyrolean chapeau. Séverine hefted the brick in her hand and tilted her head to the side, like a seasoned detective. "Why would someone who could outsmart the digital alarms and motion-activated cameras of the Grand Palais throw a brick through the window of a hat shop?"

* * * * *

We called the police. While we waited for them to arrive, we searched the internet for "Les Frigos," which turned out to be the name of a giant, dilapidated warehouse on the Left Bank of the Seine, in the thirteenth arrondissement. Originally built as a shipping warehouse for cargo boats, it had been converted into a refrigerated train station in the 1920s, a place where fruits and vegetables bound for the open-air markets in Les Halles were stored overnight. The station had been abandoned in the 1970s when the markets moved away from Les Halles to the suburbs, and then artists began squatting in the building, converting it little by little into studio space and theaters. The building had been under constant threat of demolition for years, but by the 1980s it had become so popular with local artists that protesters persuaded the city to buy it and turn it into a public arts space, which it did. Even today, the internet said, though it had been repurposed as art studios and lofts, Les Frigos retained its dilapidated character and sense of industrial abandonment; and now, some masonry-hurling maniac wanted us to go there at midnight tonight—*de minuit ce soir*.

Séverine and I argued about whether we should tell the police about the note and the proposed rendezvous. Séverine maintained that we should keep it secret, a stark reversal of her typical position in such matters. Usually, she was for law and order, letting the professionals do their work and keeping out of harm's way, but she said that she had an intuition about Benoît, that he would be hurt if we turned the cops loose. When I argued that we should tell the police everything, she found a lighter and an ashtray and set the note on fire.

I was aghast. Séverine, in her professional life, was one of the most flamboyant people I had ever met and had won renown for her daring fashion designs, but in her private life she had always been the picture of decorum. In this way, she was the diametrical opposite of Giselle, who had always maintained a prim exterior but was secretly rather wild in her behavior. For Séverine to make such a violent, albeit small, gesture was radical.

"You know, I can just tell them what the note said," I pointed out.

"You never give me credit, do you, Luke? You always have to have things your way!"

"But I don't even understand. You have a feeling that telling the police about the note will put Benoît in more danger than not telling the police? How are you and I better equipped with our feelings to deal with hostage situations than the police with their guns?"

In my job as war photographer, I often deliberately put myself in harm's way, but I still believed very strongly in playing the odds. Never run upstairs when someone's chasing you. Don't try to quick-draw a man who already has his gun out. Never light a match in the dark in a strange building. Half of staying safe is just keeping your head and being prudent, and it did not seem prudent to go to Les Frigos in the middle of the night to meet some mysterious enemy alone, nor did I see an advantage in withholding evidence from the cops.

Séverine gazed at me dewy-eyed, and in a flash it all became clear: in order to prove to me that she could be adventurous, too, that she and I could be compatible, she would arrange for us to perform heroics to save our friend Benoît, together. In fact, our little argument over this note had nothing to do with Benoît or Séverine's intuition about the police—it was about our relationship, and about Giselle. Séverine perceived that I wanted a life of thrills and danger, so she would oblige me, even join me. The only problem was that I didn't want any adventures in Paris; adventures are highly overrated, and if the world had suddenly decided to resolve conflicts peacefully and put me out of a job, I would have been overjoyed.

"Séverine, why would you want to risk your safety and maybe even your life over this?"

"For Benoît!"

"What about. . . what's your boyfriend's name?"

"Leave Eugene out of it!"

Eugene, an earnest, self-important microbiologist who worked for the French Clinical Biological Agency, lived in the wealthy suburb of Le Vésinet. True, he was handsome, rich and spent his days trying to cure cancer, but I never saw the attraction.

"The police are obviously not helping Benoît," she said. "Didn't you say you already told them that he was being held hostage, and yet what have they done about it?"

"I don't know. Maybe they've freed him already!"

"Well, someone is still throwing bricks through my window!"

"The note said nothing about Benoît!"

When the note had burned itself out, Séverine dumped the ashes into a wastebasket, and then wadded up some tissues and threw them away, too, covering the ashes.

Have you ever noticed that, once you do one thing against your better judgment, it becomes easier to do another thing against your better judgment, and then another and another, until soon you're violating the very principles of logic itself? You start out agreeing to help a friend illegally modify some computer software, and before you know it, you're hanging from a twelfth-story ledge by your fingertips or strapping dynamite to your chest: the first little misstep leads you down a thousand-mile road to perdition. It's this kind of judgment that will get you killed in combat, and, as I stared into Séverine's burnt-almond eyes, I thought it might be the kind of thing that could get you killed in downtown Paris, too. But I agreed to keep the note secret.

* * * * *

"Trouble just seems to follow you down the street, doesn't it, Monsieur Johnson?" the policeman said when he arrived. It was the same officer who had banged on my apartment door at three o'clock that morning.

"Don't you ever go to bed?" I said.

"Since crime doesn't sleep, neither do we."

"That's very romantic, but crime is not the kind of noun that requires sleep."

"The list of crimes you're associated with," he continued

smugly, "now includes criminal damage to property." He took out his notebook and started writing a description of the scene.

"I didn't do this! I was in the back room when it happened, with the owner of the shop!"

"You know, it's a strange coincidence that the morning after you're arrested for stealing a painting from the Grand Palais, you just happen to be in a shop where a brick flies through the window."

"It's not a coincidence at all! The two events are almost certainly related, but I'm the victim!"

The officer snorted, then asked Séverine and me a series of clinical and, I thought, actually insightful questions. Séverine had to think fast in order to avoid giving away clues to the note attached to the brick—the officer clearly thought the brick was more than vandalism—but she muddled through the interrogation undetected. When the officer was satisfied and had finished scribbling, he put his notebook back in the breast pocket of his overcoat.

"We've got our eyes on you, Johnson," he said.

"Thanks. Maybe you can keep me from getting hurt."

When the cop left, Séverine hugged me warmly. "Thank you, Luke. Thank you for not telling them about the note."

"You're welcome. So? Les Frigos tonight?"

"Of course," she said. She still had not let me go. "You'll see how right I am." And then she kissed me on the lips, again! And I kissed her back!

A blast of wintry air blew splinters of glass from the jagged hole in the window to the floor below, making a tinkling chime. "All right, Séverine, stop it!" I broke her embrace. "I need to take some clothes to Giselle, in jail."

"I need to call someone to fix the hole in my window." Neither of us moved. "Shall we meet at the Happy Elephant in two hours?"

Remember that thing I just said, about doing things against your better judgment? How doing one thing against your better judgment leads you down the long road to perdition?

"Sure," I said. "I'll see you there."

5

Ransom by Proxy

I traced a circuitous route from *Chapellerie Séverine* to Giselle's apartment, which took me through *Arts et Metiers*. The medieval streets were even more crowded than usual, and I gave up trying to fight for a spot on the sidewalks and instead walked directly down the middle of the avenues, hopping on and off the walkways as compact cars honked through. Snow fell in sparse, wispy flurries.

The French have a penchant for absolutism, for thinking that things are all one way or all another, which is why their politics are marked by a general inability to compromise and why they tend to hold their personal opinions until the bitter end, even after they have clearly lost an argument. The concept of a disagreement ending in a win-win compromise simply doesn't make sense for the French: in a disagreement, there must always be a winner and a loser, and this forms one of the most baffling paradoxes of French life. Their state is monolithic, their attitudes are generally inflexible and their moral sense is fixed and all-encompassing, yet their fidelity to their own personal moral standards wavers constantly. Intentional vagueness is a design feature of their language. The right thing for me to do, in my American imagination, seemed perfectly clear: tell the police everything, stay away from Séverine, and retreat to my apartment until Benoît and the painting had both been found by the proper authorities. But I had become French enough to see that Benoît's predicament might not respond to legalistic measures, that the resources of the state could not solve every problem and that I could not return to my normal life in any event until everything was settled. In the Congo, they would have found simple solutions to all of these difficulties: I would be shot by Giselle, or Séverine, or both; Jacques Martin would be shot by Benoît or Pierre Bergé, or both; Pierre Bergé would be shot by Jacques Martin, or me; Séverine would be shot by Giselle and vice versa. At the end of the Congolese solution, there would be a Hamlet-sized stack of bodies and a lot of problems solved, except, of course, that no matter who shot whom or for what reason, the painting would still be missing. You can't shoot an art theft. And anyway, the Congolese method had worked poorly for the Congolese, who were still shooting each other after several generations of such problem-solving. I had to do something, and the invitation to Les Frigos was the only idea I had. The fact that it was somebody else's idea and probably a trap did not make it any less plausible a course of action—unless I could think of something better.

I finally spotted the plain-clothes policeman who had been assigned to me when I turned down rue Saint Saveur. He was medium height, with brown hair and a cleft chin; he was wearing a black suit with a blue tie; and he was smoking a cigarette. I committed his appearance to memory and then proceeded briskly to Giselle's building.

Giselle's apartment was on the third floor of a crooked, gabled stone structure, whose windows were protected by wooden shutters painted an absurdly bright orange. The avant-garde color choice was surely influenced by the modern architecture of the Pompidou Center a few blocks away, but the particular shade of electric pumpkin slathered over the shutters did not speak well of modernity. I let myself in, climbed the stairs to her apartment and peeked out the living room window to confirm that I had, indeed, picked out the policeman who was following me: he was on the street corner below, lurking in an apartment doorway, pretending to have difficulty lighting another cigarette, surreptitiously staring up at me.

I packed an overnight bag with a change of clothes and toiletries for Giselle and was just about to leave, when I noticed that her answering machine light was blinking. I hit play and heard the gravelly voice of an old man.

"I congratulate you on your success stealing the painting. I can't believe you did it so neatly, though of course I also can't help noticing your troubles with the police, but I'm confident that you will sort that out as neatly as you did the security at the Grand Palais. I agree to your terms. I will meet your representative at Les Frigos tonight. I know that I have forced you into an uncomfortable position, and I apologize for the difficulties I have caused Benoît, but you must understand how important that painting is to me, and it is rightly mine."

The message stopped, and the light on the machine became solid red. I picked up Giselle's phone and hit the "last call return" button. The phone rang ten times before a man picked up—but it was not the same man who had left the message. I discovered that the number connected to a phone booth on the Champs-Élysées. The caller had covered his tracks by using one of the nearly extinct public phones in the *Voie Triomphale*! I sat down, hit play again and tried to figure out what was happening.

It seemed that the caller must have been Jacques Martin, who apparently believed that Giselle had stolen *The Despair of Pierrot*. And he believed that Giselle had contacted him suggesting a rendezvous at Les Frigos. But then, if Martin thought Giselle had the painting and Bergé thought Martin had it, who had thrown the brick through Séverine's shop window, also demanding a meeting tonight at Les Frigos?

Who actually had the painting? And who was arranging the rendezvous? Someone was setting Martin up and using us to do it.

I looked out at the man who had followed me from Séverine's shop. He had finally lit his cigarette and was now on the near side of the street, pretending to look at a pocket metro map. Perhaps he wasn't a cop, after all. I erased the message.

* * * * *

When I left Giselle's apartment, I walked directly up to the malingering metro-map man and asked who he was and why he had been following me. He pretended not to have been following me and asked for directions on his map, which I gave him. I watched him walk away toward Beaubourg—he did not look back—and then I headed toward the Les Halles police station.

When you're used to being in dangerous situations, you develop a sixth sense about your surroundings, about where possible enemies might be lurking, how many steps it will take to reach the next corner on a dead run, the best hiding places if bullets start to fly; and though I was feeling strung out from my sleepless night, the outlines of buildings along the avenue were so sharp and clear they almost hurt my eyes. I sized up every man's stubbly chin and every woman's lined lips with barely controlled paranoia, yet I saw nothing suspicious on the way to the police station. It could have been the most ordinary day in the history of the world.

Inside the police station, I picked out the officer who had come to Séverine's shop, sitting at a desk punching away at a computer keyboard, using just his index fingers to type. His hands were jerking wildly back and forth, like the front legs of a poisoned insect. As I passed his station toward the holding cells, he gave a jaunty flip of his head and a superior smirk, as if to say that I myself would be occupying one of the cells soon, and then he went back to his neurotoxic typing.

I filled out a Request for Visit form, had the form reviewed and stamped and was told that Giselle was already in the Visitors' Pen with someone else. I was then forced to empty the contents of Giselle's overnight bag and my own pockets into a plastic tub, after which I was led through a series of electronically locked doors and stairways to the basement, where I was searched again.

The Visitors' Pen was a large, canary yellow rectangle with a single horizontal red stripe painted halfway up every wall. The room was divided down the center by a thick metal half-wall that came up to my waist; on top of this divider, a long transparent Plexiglas panel had been affixed, and tables and chairs had been aimed at the Plexiglas. On one side sat prisoners, on the other sat visitors. Each visitor station was separated from the others by low wooden partitions: while seated, each visitor could see only the prisoner directly opposite, but the guards standing on either end could still look down into every station at once. There were also video cameras at every corner, placed up high near the ceiling. Tiny holes had been drilled into the Plexiglas above each table, in the pattern of a microphone, so that prisoners and visitors could speak through them.

When I entered, I saw Giselle at the far end of the pen, seated across from her nineteen-year-old daughter Manon. Manon was perched at the edge of her chair and was leaning right up to the glass, and when she turned to me, she looked as if she had just discovered a rat hair in her crème caramel.

Manon Orliac was skinny and frail-looking, with long brown hair tousled around an elfin face. Her eyes were flecked silver-blue and gray, like the crushed glass in marbles. She had been estranged from Giselle and her father for most of her young life and had been raised by her grandparents, but she and Giselle had reconciled recently and their relationship was now almost closer than that of a more traditional mother and daughter, since they had developed a profound need for one another during their estrangement. Since entering the University of Paris, Manon had become one of the "family regulars" at the Happy Elephant, often bringing her classwork there in the afternoons, to study over espressos and *pain au chocolat* before Jean-Pierre opened for business in the evenings.

Having been abandoned as a small child by both parents at separate times and in different ways, Manon had an extremely complex attitude toward authority, and her sympathies swung unpredictably between strict law-and-order and social-anarchy. She stuttered, and her speech impediment betrayed a deep existential anxiety about her place in the world and her inability to trust others; when she couldn't get a word out properly, her stutter made her seem volatile and furious, even when she was just trying to make a joke.

Since I had been with Giselle, I had grown closer and closer to Manon, and I thought of her as a precocious niece, if not exactly a daughter. I saw now, from the look on her face, that she could not decide whether to be exasperated on her mother's behalf, amused at the absurd injustice of the whole predicament or disgusted by the whole State of France.

"Luke," Giselle said. "Thank God! Would you tell her that this is all a big misunderstanding?"

I kissed Manon on both cheeks and sat down beside her. "I'd like to," I said. "But I don't think it is."

Manon clucked. "Are you saying that *m-m-maman* did steal that p-painting?"

"Of course not, but it's not a misunderstanding. We've

been framed, so whoever framed us understood exactly what they were doing. I had assumed that it was Jacques Martin framing us because of something Benoît had done thirty years ago, but now I'm not so sure." I told them what had happened at Séverine's shop. The wheels behind Manon's eyes tried to mill out a solution. "There's more to it than that," I told Manon. "But I'll have to catch you up on the whole story somewhere more private." I then told Giselle that I had left her overnight bag upstairs with the bailiff and that the police would give it to her when they had catalogued its contents.

"What are you going to do now?" Giselle said.

"For one thing, I'm going to get you out of here before they decide to put you in a real prison on some trumped-up charge. For another, I'm going to find Jacques Martin. I'm pretty sure the police have someone following me now, so all I really have to do is find Martin and yell 'help,' and they'll grab him. Then maybe we can get to the bottom of this."

"Do you have any idea where he is?"

"As a matter of fact, I know just where he'll be tonight, and he'll probably bring Benoît with him." I nodded toward the guards. "I'll have to tell you about that later, too."

I made sure that Giselle was doing well and didn't need any other assistance, and then we all said our goodbyes. Manon and I made our way back upstairs. On the way out, I stopped to talk with the officer who seemed to be in charge of my case.

"Hey, do you have someone following me?"

"We're certainly keeping tabs on you," he smirked. I wondered if smirking frequently in the civil service put you on the fast track to promotion.

"Well, if the guy following me is about 1.5 meters tall, handsome, brown hair, medium build with a cleft chin and is wearing a black suit with blue socks and a blue tie today, could you please tell him to be more careful?"

He spread his arms and raised his eyebrows to indicate ignorance. "I don't know anyone like that," he said. "Our friend Pissoux was tailing you this morning and an officer in a wheelchair will watch you this afternoon. I'll tell them to be careful tonight." He winked, and I wondered what he meant by "tonight," if he already knew about Les Frigos.

Manon and I left the police station and walked toward the Happy Elephant in silence. She stared at the side of my head all the way to the bar, waiting for an explanation, and I kept putting my hand up, asking her to be patient till we could speak freely; but she continued to stare nevertheless.

* * * * *

Séverine was already at the Happy Elephant, sitting on a barstool opposite Jean-Pierre. I walked in first and she threw her arms around my neck before she saw Manon coming in behind me, and she stiffened. I caught Manon's eye—it was obvious that she sensed something had happened between Séverine and me. Even Jean-Pierre raised his eyebrows at this thawing of our Cold War, and now Manon and Jean-Pierre waited not just to hear my story about the painting but also for an explanation about me and Séverine.

I broke Séverine's embrace, locked the Happy Elephant's front door and indicated a table at the back of the bar. "Let's relax for a while," I said loudly, for the benefit of the guys outside in a theoretical police sound truck.

Though it was still fairly early in the day, I asked Jean-Pierre for a glass of armagnac: he obliged with a snifter and then brewed espressos for everyone else. When we were all seated comfortably with our beverages—Manon across from Séverine, spraying imaginary green paint across Séverine's fox-fur hat—I dropped my voice to a faint whisper and told everyone everything that had happened since Giselle had arrived at the AAC fundraising dinner the evening before. Jean-Pierre was encouraged that Benoît, apparently, was safe for the moment and that we knew where he would probably be that evening, the bait for a supposed ransom exchange. If Martin followed through with his promise and showed his face at Les Frigos, we could at least try to rescue Benoît, whatever else happened.

"But this brick through the window disturbs me," Jean-Pierre said, petting his beard. "Obviously, Martin didn't throw the brick, since he left that message on Giselle's answering machine. In fact, Martin thinks that Giselle called him to arrange the meeting at Les Frigos! So let's ask ourselves: who would be in a position to know that Séverine was involved in this mess in the first place, and who would want Martin to go to Les Frigos tonight for a ransom swap?"

"And why would they invite us along?" I said.

"Well, we know that someone is following Luke," Séverine said. "He followed him from my shop to Giselle's apartment, right? That same person could have thrown the brick."

"Maybe," I said. "But I think the guy following me was a policeman. No criminal worth his salt would have allowed himself to be spotted so easily. It's possible that he wanted me to spot him, that the police were making sure I knew that I was being watched. And I don't think the police would break Séverine's window, even as a tactic." I took a meditative drink of armagnac. "To me, the most important question is, who has the painting? Not Jacques Martin, apparently. Not Pierre Bergé. Not the Grand Palais. Yet Martin thinks that he's going to get the painting tonight at Les Frigos, and whoever threw the brick must know that."

"Maybe the person who threw the brick actually does have the painting," said Séverine. "If he knows the police are following you, he could make sure the painting is at Les Frigos when you arrive, and that would give the police the criminal grounds to lock you up."

"But it doesn't really make sense to frame me for the theft," I said. "If he has the painting, he can sell it or keep it or whatever. What interest would this person have in framing me or Giselle, and why would he take the risk of stealing the painting in the first place, if he were just going to use it as bait to even some score? To steal a painting from the Grand Palais is no mean feat, and now everyone in France knows that the painting was stolen, and the police are looking everywhere for it. To put yourself at that kind of risk, you have to actually want the painting for itself, I think, because there are a million easier ways to get revenge." I stared into the amber liquid in my glass, hoping an answer would rise magically to the surface. "Besides, the mystery person who threw the brick didn't instigate these events—Jacques Martin did, by kidnapping Benoît, and we know why Martin wants the painting."

Manon said, "I think B-B-Benoît is the k-key."

"Given the potential danger that Benoît is in," said Jean-Pierre, "I believe that our obligation is to tell the police about Les Frigos."

Silence. Everyone looked down at the table.

"What difference does it make who stole the painting?" Jean-Pierre went on. "Or who has the painting now? Our only interest is making sure that Benoît is safe. The painting has nothing to do with us."

"Except," I said, "that it's still possible that Giselle and I will end up in jail for stealing it. For instance, could it be possible that whoever has the painting will keep it and will also make sure the police find some evidence to hold me or Giselle or Benoît for the theft?"

Séverine said, "But the police can't arrest you for mentioning the painting at a dinner party! That's the only evidence that exists, that you said '*The Despair of Pierrot*' to Pierre at the Godenot Gallery."

I slumped back in my chair. "Someone is being framed, for some reason, and until we discover who and for what, it's not clear to me what the police will do or what's truly at stake. Any person who's clever enough to steal a painting from the Grand Palais is also clever enough to incriminate us, if revenge is the dish being served here."

"But revenge for what?" Jean-Pierre said.

"Exactly," I replied. I drained off my drink and got up to pour myself another.

"M-maybe there's a c-c-clue in the p-painting itself."

"You mean hidden in the canvas somewhere?" said Jean-Pierre.

"No, in the theme of the p-painting. Has anyone seen it?"

"I saw a picture of it on television," Jean-Pierre said.

While I searched beneath the bar for Jean-Pierre's private stock of Dartigalongue 1945, I recited what Bergé had said about the painter James Ensor, about his use of burlesque themes to comment on modern life. I unstoppered a bottle of the rare armagnac and poured two fingers into my snifter, swirled it and inhaled the rich aromas of oak and vanilla. I raised the glass in a toast and said, "I guess I should call Joseph Danton. If anyone would know about *The Despair of Pierrot*, it would be him."

"I know something about P-Pierrot, the character," Manon offered. "P-Pierrot is a stock figure from C-C-Commedia dell'Arte." Her eyes flashed at the difficult consonants. "He's often in l-love with the beautiful C-Columbina, and he always loses her to Harlequin."

Manon went on to describe the typical plots of Commedia dell'Arte—a medieval form of theater that originated in Italy and then spread throughout Europe with the Renaissance. In Commedia dell'Arte, the same characters show up over and over again in plays with the loose structure of boy-meets-girl boy-loses-girl boy-gets-girl-back. In most of the shows, the action revolves around a pair of lovers who want to marry but are thwarted by a complication, either a third person, who forms a love triangle with the first two, or by elders who object to the marriage. The actors play out scenes that are largely improvised, but everyone in the audience knows more or less how the play will end, with a happy marriage—sort of like a medieval situation comedy where the actors make up the dialogue but the plot is the same every week. The pleasure of Commedia dell'Arte comes from the cleverness of the improvisations and the actors' physical stunts and pratfalls. The audience can always easily identify the characters because they wear masks and colorful costumes that correspond to their roles, and the actors always play the roles for laughs, most of which involve ribaldry. Although the plays end happily, in the love triangle variations one of the lovers always loses out, and Manon theorized that any painting called *The Despair of Pierrot* would be about the eternal sadness of the character who never gets the girl. "So it p-probably p-p-portrays the underlying grief in the c-comedy, the heartache of the jilted l-l-lover."

"Seems like a dubious keepsake for either Martin or Bergé," I said. "I don't think I'd want a painting of an eternally jilted lover to commemorate being jilted. It's just too sad."

"Unless it's worth two million euros," Jean-Pierre said.

Séverine got up, came over to the bar and cupped her hands to my ear, so that the others could not hear, "And what about us, then, Luke? Am I acting the role of Pierrot in this little drama?"

Though no one else could make out her exact words,

the gist of the message was clear to Manon, who stood up so quickly that she knocked over her chair. "M-maybe we should go see Joseph D-Danton together, Luke!"

I drained the entire glass of vintage armagnac. I did not feel like acting the role of Columbina in some gender-confused revival of a medieval burlesque. "Sure. Let's all go see Danton together," I said sarcastically. "That'll make him very happy! But first, I'm going to bed."

I was so exhausted I felt sick. I kissed everyone's cheeks in turn and told Jean-Pierre to put the expensive hooch on my tab. "I'll call Danton," I said. "I'll try to set up a meeting at the Orsay this afternoon. Keep your cell phones on, and I'll let you know time and place. And be advised that as soon as I tell you anything by cell, the cops will know it, too. Whatever else happens, let's meet back here this evening at nine and make a plan for Les Frigos. And do not, under any circumstances, mention Les Frigos if we talk by phone!"

I stepped out onto rue des Tournelles and shut the door behind me. The temperature had dropped below freezing and a light swirling snow was falling steadily now, though the flakes melted as soon as they touched the ground.

I walked back to my apartment and telephoned Joseph Danton's office at the Orsay. His assistant took my message that I urgently needed to meet with him, and then I dialed his cell, which he did not answer. I imagined that it would be a long time before he was happy to hear from me again, but I left a voicemail briefly explaining the situation, hoping that he would see the potential promise in helping me recover *Pierrot*. I set my alarm clock to ring in three hours, flopped into bed fully clothed and fell immediately into a deep sleep.

6

A LESSON IN ART HISTORY

I awoke to insistent pounding on my apartment door fifteen minutes before my alarm was set to go off. I dragged myself out of bed and peered blearily through the peephole: Manon stood in the hall, arms akimbo.

"You look t-terrible," she said, when I opened the door.

"Everybody's a critic."

She strode purposefully into the room, tossed her bag onto a chair and sat down on the edge of my bed, posture perfectly erect. Manon had spent much of her youth hiding from her family troubles by reading books, and her curiosity was almost as vibrant a part of her character as her anger. She was still just a teenager, but she was scholarly, and like many young people who have been abused, she was a pudding of immaturity and precocious wisdom that had not yet set into a stable mold. It was never clear, when speaking with her, if you were talking to the gum-chewing video game enthusiast or the world-weary intellectual consumed by ennui. She had become acutely perceptive emotionally as a defense against disappointment and abandonment, but she did not always know how to react to the complex situations that she accurately diagnosed.

"If you won't t-tell m-my mother, would you at least t-t-tell me?"

"Tell you what?"

"About Séverine."

My brain felt spun from cotton candy. I yawned. "What about Séverine?"

Manon stared at me poker-faced, silently calling my bluff. I yawned again. Exactly what had happened? Nothing, I thought. Séverine and I had kissed in a moment of confusion and stress, apparently because Séverine was intent on forcing me to deal with the messy conclusion of our relationship two years after it had actually ended.

"Nothing's happened," I finally said. "She's friends with Pierre Bergé. Bergé knew that she knew me, and he called her to arrange a meeting between us. That's all. She's mixed up in this business with the painting because of her former professional relationship with Yves Saint Laurent and her friendship with Benoît. It's just a big mess."

"The p-painting is m-m-meaningless. I know how c-complex love affairs can be, Luke. I know my m-mother."

"The painting won't seem so meaningless when it lands us all in the clink." I ran my fingers through my hair and felt the hedgerow of whiskers on my cheek. Someone should design a business suit you can sleep in.

"You n-never thought of getting back together with Séverine?"

I shrugged and went into the kitchen. Manon followed me and stood in the doorway, while I filled the kettle with water and turned on the hotplate. She helped herself to a stale biscuit.

"I don't know why it's your business," I said.

"It's not. But m-maybe I like you and I don't like seeing you do stupid things. Maybe I w-w-want you to stay with my m-mother."

"All right. But this conversation stays in strict confidence between you and me."

"D'accord. M-motus et bouche cousue." She mimed zipping her lips.

"Nothing has really happened, anyway, like I said. Honestly. It's just a ghost from my past with Séverine."

"It didn't seem like a ghost to me. In the b-bar."

"We kissed. That's all. At her shop. It happened in a moment of real turmoil. You know, Bergé was there in the shop and he was extremely volatile, shouting and throwing things around, and I'd just stood up to a police interrogation all night. Séverine kissed me, and I let her, a little too long. I was just overwhelmed."

Manon laughed. "So you k-kissed right in front of Bergé?"

"Practically. That's why he stormed out of the shop. Then someone threw a brick through the window. That's all. Now Séverine, as usual, is over-thinking everything, and she's using her accidental involvement with this painting to force an issue between us, to make me settle accounts."

"You don't give her enough c-credit. So she k-k-kissed you first?"

"Yes. But I could have stopped it and didn't. And then we kissed again later, and the lines got blurrier."

Manon tsk-tsked.

My cell phone rang and, to my relief, it was Joseph Danton calling to tell me that he could educate me about James Ensor, but considering what he called "the delicate situation," he would have to insist on doing it in person, and he had time right then and only right then. I would have to go to the Orsay immediately. "Next time, why don't you take a class?" he said viciously. "I can't give you basic lectures in art history every time you get in trouble."

"I didn't do this," I said. "Why are you angry at me?"

"You always seem to be involved in something that's 'not your fault,' Luke. At some point, though, something is somebody's fault."

The phone went dead. I wondered if perhaps Danton thought I really might have stolen the painting, even though he was my alibi for the night of the theft. In any event, Danton still blamed me for costing his charity a big donation from Bergé, whether I had stolen the Ensor or not. Nevertheless, he was willing to hedge his bets, to help me in order to possibly bring some of Bergé's auction money to the AAC; not to mention the fact that, as a relatively important member of the French Ministry of Culture, Danton had something personal at stake in recovering a major artwork stolen from the Grand Palais.

The kettle whistled and I asked Manon to make coffee. I went into the bathroom and turned on the shower. "Do you really want to go to the Orsay with me?" I said. I stripped out of my clothes and stepped into the tub. The hot water melted my cotton candy thoughts into a tangled mess of pink circus slop swirling giddily down the drain.

"Yes, I'll go," said Manon. "G-give me two minutes and I'll c-come back with bread."

I heard my apartment door open and close, and I stood letting the hot water wash over me. Slowly, the fog in my mind materialized externally in the steam, and I watched it cloud my bathroom and fog my mirror and coalesce in little droplets the color of caramel on my grimy ceiling. By the time I turned off the water and stepped out into the chilly kitchen, I could almost think clearly again. I sipped the coffee Manon had made and called Séverine and Jean-Pierre, to ask if they wanted to come along to the museum. Séverine was obliged to stay at her shop to deal with the man replacing her glass, and Jean-Pierre said, falsely, "I have to open the Elephant."

I finished drying my hair, found a clean suit in the closet and stared out at the gossamer snowflakes wafting gently into my courtyard.

* * * * *

On the metro, Manon told me that her mother had had many clandestine affairs with men over the years; that, in fact, most of Giselle's life had been clandestine while Manon had been growing up. Giselle had been desperately trying to live up to her parents' expectations, to make the family antique shop more profitable than it had ever been before, but she was temperamentally unsuited to such a cultured, respectable existence. Every choice Giselle had made before settling into a relationship with me had been a mistake, in Manon's opinion, including the choice to give birth to Manon herself—Manon believed that her mother had sabotaged her entire life and happiness by being untrue to herself, and this sabotage had destroyed not only her work and her family life, but her love life as well. Manon had witnessed the many destructive affairs that her mother had had with married men, chance sexual encounters that had "just happened," that were desperate attempts to escape reality rather than build healthy relationships. Manon believed that her mother was happy for the first time in her life now that she had a job in someone else's shop and a solid relationship with me, and she did not want to see me destroy that relationship for idiotic reasons, for something that "just happened" with Séverine.

"If nothing else, Luke," she said, "think of m-me. Think of m-my relationship with my m-mother. The time she's been with you has b-been the only t-t-time we've ever known each other as p-people, really, and you should c-consider what's at stake for everyone. For me."

I sighed. One moment of weakness with my ex-girlfriend and I was risking Manon's relationship with her mother! It was too much weight to lay on an incidental kiss, I thought, and I had more pressing things to worry about.

I kissed Manon on the forehead. "The last thing I want

is to cause a rift between you and your mother. Or between me and your mother. Or between you and me, for that matter. But Séverine may complicate matters on her own, if she's so inclined."

"It takes t-two to t-t-tango, Luke."

The subway car pulled into the Tuileries station, and we joined the throng pressing up the stairs. "One thing at a time, all right? Let's see what Danton can tell us. Maybe you're right, and there's some clue in the painting itself that will help us."

* * * * *

Because Paris is an ancient city, many of its downtown buildings have been reincarnated from earlier failures. The *Musée d'Orsay*, for example was built as a train station at the turn of the twentieth century, then became a hotel, and is now the world's primary warehouse of Impressionist paintings. From the outside, as you approach it across the Seine from the Jardin des Tuileries, the building still offers the imposing grandeur of a nineteenth century *gare*, with two extraordinarily beautiful clock towers facing the river, both of which tell the same time (a rarity among public clocks downtown).

It was almost dark at just after four o'clock in the afternoon, and we crossed the Seine on the Passerelle Léopold-Sédar-Senghor. Snow was falling faster and wetter now, and the river's usual fetid green looked strangely dark and gray, as it accepted the heavy snowflakes falling like tiny white pieces of debris from a massive detonation a hundred kilometers away. It rarely snows in Paris and rarely sticks to the ground when it does, but today the temperature was falling nearly as fast as the snow, and a glaze of white frosted the stone benches on the bridge.

The Orsay was closing for the day as we arrived, but

tourists were still milling in the plaza north of the entrance, looking quizzically at maps or having their photos taken while they leaned jauntily against statuary. We walked in and explained our errand to a navy-coated museum attendant, who phoned Danton and conducted a perfunctory, irritated search of Manon's bag. We passed through metal detectors and walked into the glass-domed main gallery, past a series of bucolic Pissarros, to a staircase that led to the administrative suite on the third floor.

Danton greeted us at the door to his office, and we stepped inside. I always found it curious that Danton did not decorate his personal spaces with art—neither his office nor his apartment featured a single painting on any of the walls— and he preferred spare, sleek, black and white furniture in the Swedish style. Of course, his workplace, just outside his office, contained gilt-framed paintings by nearly every important European painter of the nineteenth century, so he might justly consider decorating his own office redundant.

On the conference table in the corner of the office, Danton had set up a laptop computer and a projector, which he had aimed at a bare wall. He directed us to take seats at the table.

"I want to show you something," he said. "A video that the BRB just sent over." The BRB was the *Brigade de Répression du Banditisme*, a special elite corps of the police under the command of the Interior Ministry, which was charged with solving art thefts.

"So BRB is involved?"

"What did you expect? Here, watch. It's the surveillance video from the Grand Palais security cameras at the moment the James Ensor was stolen."

He dimmed the lights using a remote control and punched a key on his laptop. The projector threw an image up on the wall, an image that looked like a photograph of an especially plush, over-decorated bedroom.

"This is one of the exhibits they opened to the public as a prelude to the auction," Danton said. "They re-created Yves Saint Laurent's bedroom from his home on rue de Babylone, which is where *The Despair of Pierrot* was hanging when he died."

"Th-that was his b-b-bedroom?!"

Saint Laurent's bedroom looked like a museum storeroom already, it was so jam-packed with extraordinary art, sculpture and antique furniture. Even I recognized some of the paintings he had collected, they were so famous. It was staggering, and this room was just one of many rooms in just one of his many homes.

"You can see why this collection is so important, and why so much attention has been paid to the auction," said Danton. "This is one of the most significant private collections of art in the world and includes works from the Middle Ages to 2008. It's comprehensive, tasteful and rare." Danton pointed to *The Despair of Pierrot*, in the corner of the projected image, where it was hanging over a boudoir table. "This Ensor is one of many transitional works Saint Laurent owned, works that are pivotal in the development of important styles or movements. Many of the paintings are both extraordinary art in themselves and cultural milestones."

We continued to watch the projected video for more than a minute. Nothing happened. It looked for all the world like a still photograph of Saint Laurent's empty bedroom at night.

"What does this tell us?" I said.

Danton put his hand up for me to wait. Another thirty seconds elapsed before *The Despair of Pierrot* simply disappeared from the wall. Danton held a key down on his laptop, and the video rewound. He played it again: there was no warning, no movement either in the gallery or of the camera, not even an obvious splice when the camera might have been stopped and then restarted. One second the painting was there, the next it was gone, like magic.

"For a period of approximately ninety seconds, this camera was feeding a recorded image into the surveillance network, not an image of the gallery in real time. What we have just watched is the same still image for ninety seconds in a row. Someone took that camera offline long enough to take the painting from the wall without being detected, but neither the RMN nor the BRB nor the Police Nationale is sure how it was done, technically. This individual camera does not record independently from the system as a whole, so the tampering had to have occurred within the main control board, or it had to affect every single camera feed in the Grand Palais."

"And no alarm sounded, correct?" I said. "Meaning that someone also disabled the alarm system."

"Disabled or bypassed."

"Do the alarms and the security cameras share common circuits or control panels?"

"None, other than the electrical grid itself."

"So they must be thinking it's an inside job," I said.

"That's the obvious line of inquiry," said Danton. "So far, the guards are clean. They've all passed lie detector tests, and as far as the BRB can tell, every guard was where he was supposed to be when the theft occurred. The time stamps taken from security camera images all match the actual, accurate times that they should display, except for that ninety second window when no new image came from that single camera."

"So it was someone manning the main board."

"Possibly, but there's no evidence to indicate that and the guard on the main control board passed his lie detector."

"And nothing at all suspicious appears on any of the other cameras? For instance, no one in a black suit running down a hall with a painting?"

"No other movement in the entire Grand Palais, except for guards making their rounds."

"And where is that room in the Grand Palais, the bedroom re-creation that held the Ensor?"

"In the Nave. There's a glass tower in the gallery above it, and there's one basement room below. The painting simply could not have been lifted out through the glass tower, so the two real options for the thief were the Entrée Clemenceau on Avenue du General-Eisenhower or the basement, where there's an alarmed emergency exit beneath the Palais de la Decouverte."

"Maybe it's a trick, and the painting is still in the Grand Palais somewhere waiting to be taken out," I said. "Perhaps it will be taken out at the auction, as part of the packaging of another painting, for example."

Danton frowned at me. "Unlikely, given Christie's protocols, though I will pass your theory along to the BRB. They are already searching the building with a fine-toothed comb." He punched another key on the laptop, and the image disappeared. Then he opened another computer application and typed in some information. "Let me show you this presentation about James Ensor. We curated an exhibit of his works last year and put together this audio-visual tour."

Manon and I settled in for our crash course on Ensor. Like many of his contemporaries working in high art in the late nineteenth and early twentieth centuries, Ensor started off as a fairly traditional academic artist and then spun further and further away from conventional forms. Early in his career, he experimented with Impressionism, becoming one of Belgium's most celebrated artists by the 1880s. Soon, he became bored with paint and began creating massive charcoal and pencil sketches, some as large as eight feet tall and twelve feet across, attempting to convince the art world that pencil could be as important a medium as paint. No one endorsed this idea, however, and Ensor fell into disrepute with the critics. He then returned to paint and became one of the founding members of an avant-garde group called Les Vingt (the Twenty), experimenting with light and form, moving increasingly toward abstract works in which the paint itself and patterns of color were the subjects. He finally settled into a mode of allegorical paintings that fell somewhere between representation and pure fancy, paintings that often featured the artist himself being martyred at the hands of his critics.

"Ensor had many enemies in the art world of Ostend in particular and Belgium in general," a woman's voice-over narration said through the computer's speakers. "And he took revenge on them for their disapproval of his work by painting them into his allegories, portraying his critics and other artists as historical, biblical or mythical figures and viciously attacking them through parody or juxtaposition. Many of his most scathing commentaries are incomprehensible to modern viewers unfamiliar with the relatively obscure world of Belgian art criticism."

"Sounds like a fun guy," I said. Manon shushed me.

We learned that, despite his incredible egotism and personal pettiness, Ensor was extraordinarily talented at representing light, and his techniques influenced many Expressionists, as they created the increasingly abstract painting styles that would dominate the first half of the twentieth century. He was one of the earliest artists to consider paint itself, as it appears on a canvas, to be valid subject matter.

"Ensor's striking use of carnival masks, burlesque figures and theatrical characters to comment on death," the female narrator continued, "also anticipated the increasingly morbid preoccupations of European art after World War One." The virtual tour showed us a series of Ensor's works portraying death as a skeleton at a masquerade ball, death attending an otherwise festive carnival, and scenes of everyday work being performed by skeletons. The colors of these paintings, in contrast to their themes, were vibrant, light and happy, often using bright blues, reds and pinks that bordered on pastel—colors that were so luminous that light seemed to be shining from inside the paint itself.

Finally, we saw a series of carnival and burlesque paintings in which Commedia dell'Arte characters portrayed scenes of buffoonery tinged with sadness, as characters mocked one another cruelly or broke down in obvious pain and misery before an entire company's jeers. *The Despair of Pierrot* appeared in this final series, and Danton stopped the show, to let us linger on it.

A grimacing, orange-haired man with sunken eyes, Pierrot was dressed in a clown costume, a blowzy white cape with blue trim. The cape had big blue balls for buttons, running down the front, making him seem like a cross between a medieval jester wracked with emotional pain and a petulant schoolboy in silly pajamas made to go to bed without dessert. He stood on a poorly defined blue-green hillside—more a swirling swath of color than a true representation of a hill. In fact, the only clues that the scene took place on a landscape at all were a tiny windmill off in the distance and an absurdly large white cloud billowing up behind the hill, but these details were completely fabulist, unlike any actual hillside or sky that had ever existed, and they seemed meant to suggest a mood of turmoil rather than anything real. Dancing around Pierrot on this abstract hillside, other Commedia dell'Arte characters wearing masks and heavy theatrical facepaint mocked Pierrot in his suffering. Completely disembodied masks, with no apparent wearers, floated around Pierrot's head, suggesting that the entire scene could be taking place in his own mind, that it was the painful memory of these characters that tormented him. Pierrot was unmistakably not the "sad clown" of the Ringling Brothers circus, who uses his apparent heartache only to get laughs and then becomes miraculously happy as the show ends—Pierrot's misery was real and his alienation from the happy-go-lucky characters floating around him unmistakable. *The Despair of Pierrot* was a portrayal of bleak isolation and loneliness, and it was moving even as a projected image on a white office wall. The happy colors—peach, blue, gold, green, bright yellow and red—served to illustrate the happiness all around Pierrot that he could not participate in.

"I still can't imagine how this painting can sum up a philosophy of love," I said. "That's what Bergé said it represented for him and Saint Laurent."

"M-maybe they're m-more romantic than you," said Manon. "To l-love is to suffer."

"Tell that to your mother," I said.

Danton chimed in. "The Pierrot character's whole purpose in Commedia dell'Arte is to provide the romantic foil, the obstacle to true happiness that must be overcome in order for Harlequin and Columbina to marry. The suffering of Pierrot in this painting is a projection of Ensor's, which is a personal interpretation of the drama that probably would never have occurred to anyone in Renaissance Italy. This painting, in its context from late nineteenth century Belgium, is as much a statement of political and artistic dispossession as unrequited love, and it has been interpreted as everything from a proletarian indictment of bourgeois society to a portrait of Ensor's own failure to win the approval of his contemporary Belgian critics. Because Ensor often portrayed himself as Christ, it has occasionally been seen as a portrait of Ensor/Christ: notice that there are twelve figures surrounding Pierrot. Of course,

Ensor himself was neither a Marxist nor a Christian in any traditional sense, and his own government eventually awarded him the *Légion d'Honneur*, so his self-perception as an artistic martyr is more emotional than real. The artist's image of himself complicates the interpretation of these symbols."

Danton closed his laptop, and the projector went blank. He clicked the remote control and the lights in his office brightened once again.

"I believe," Danton went on, "that this painting is a powerful statement of loneliness and that a person betrayed in love could find great solace in it. I also think it's possible that a gay man could find a compelling statement of estrangement from mainstream society in its portrayal of the impossibility of finding a fulfilling love. After all, Commedia dell'Arte makes Pierrot's love for Columbina into a joke, the same way mainstream society makes gay love into a joke or a grotesque. It requires no great stretch of the imagination to think that Jacques Martin, Pierre Bergé and Yves Saint Laurent could all find something deeply personal and sentimental to share in this painting, and that they might use it as a token of affection."

I had seen and heard nothing that told us anything practical about the men wrapped up in this drama, nor could I find any clues to the likely thief in this presentation. At least, I could now recognize the painting, in the event that whoever had it really did bring it to Les Frigos tonight.

"What do you know about Pierre Bergé as a person?" I asked Danton.

"Little more than you do, probably. He's notoriously private."

Danton sat against the edge of his conference table and put one foot on the chair in front of him. He clasped his hands behind his neck and stared at the ceiling, an uncharacteristically outward sign of fatigue. It occurred to me that a great deal might be at stake for Danton in this fiasco, beyond the monetary contribution that Bergé might give *L'Association des Amis du Congo*. In his role as Curator of the Orsay, he was deeply involved with the *Réunion des Musées Nationaux* and had to serve the overarching bureaucracy in charge of all of France's museums. His tangential involvement in this theft could place him under a great deal of internal pressure from the French administration. The security systems of every museum in France were also, no doubt, being scrutinized in light of this theft, and Danton himself might have fallen under suspicion because of his association with me, however accidental my involvement in the whole affair had been. It had probably been a difficult couple of days for Danton.

"I can tell you that Bergé is shrewd, calculating and ruthless," he continued. "His words often carry multiple layers of meanings, or hide meanings cleverly, or simply obscure the truth, when it's convenient to him."

"You're saying he's a liar?"

"I'm saying that no one builds a billion dollar empire by saying exactly what he means all the time, and Bergé is keenly aware that whoever has his painting also has more on his mind than just that canvas. Think of it this way: Jacques Martin arrives at his door just before this auction demanding a keepsake of Martin's amorous life with Yves Saint Laurent. That's irritating enough. When Bergé refuses to give the painting to Martin, it disappears. Even more irritating! And now the publicity surrounding the theft has opened Bergé's and Saint Laurent's somewhat sordid past up to prurient public scrutiny once again, at a time when Bergé wants only to be celebrated as a philanthropist and add extra layers of mythology to Saint Laurent's legacy.

"But that's not all! It's possible that this theft will actually add value to the auction as a whole, since it already has become a scandalous event. The sudden wide interest in *The Despair of Pierrot* will no doubt increase its price, if it's ever recovered. Bergé knows all of this, and it's possible that he's playing an angle, pandering to the press, playing the victim to gain public sympathy, just as James Ensor used to portray himself as a martyr in his own paintings. Is Bergé a saintly philanthropist or a calculating capitalist, a bitter cuckold, a parasite still feeding on Yves Saint Laurent's fame and wealth? Will he blame the Grand Palais for the disappearance of the painting as a way of exculpating himself from a torrid love triangle that lasted thirty years, or is he genuinely distraught to be reminded of the decades-long failure of his romantic relationship with Saint Laurent, whether they were married on Saint Laurent's deathbed or not?

"Rhetorically," Danton continued, "this situation is extremely complex from Bergé's point of view, and it's unclear how he sees it or how it will ultimately affect his reputation and the proceeds from the auction. It's a delicate case, but my advice to you is: trust that Bergé is completely aware of the complexities involved, and his real interests might be different from his apparent ones."

"So you think his volatile behavior might be an act?"

"No," Danton said. "Bergé has always been known for violent outbursts. I merely caution you not to think of him as one-dimensional or easily pegged. Know that his defining characteristic as a businessman is his ability to manipulate the people around him, often so that they don't even know that they're doing his bidding." He checked his watch. "Now," he said sternly, "I'll have to ask you to leave. The Inspector General for Cultural Affairs is bringing his team here for an emergency meeting, and I don't believe he would think favorably of your presence."

As irritated as Danton was with me, he was still trying to

help me in the best way he knew how, by giving me information and support, even though it put him in an awkward position. On the other hand, I thought, he had probably broadcast our entire meeting through hidden microphones to agents of the BRB, who no doubt knew that I was in Danton's office. It was a quintessentially French moment: Danton blamed me for costing his charity money, though Danton himself was my alibi for the evening the painting was stolen; he seemed genuine in his desire to help me, and he had been under no obligation to invite me and Manon to the Orsay, yet in doing so he might also be helping the French government convict me, in the event that I really had masterminded the theft. Telling me his inside opinions about Pierre Bergé could possibly help me stay out of trouble with the police and Bergé, yet doing so could betray whatever confidence Bergé might ultimately place in Danton, which would undoubtedly cost Danton's charity any hope of receiving a donation from the auction. By inviting Manon and me here for this tête-à-tête, Danton had both helped me and kept tabs on me for the French government, and he had both potentially compromised and increased the AAC's chances of a large donation. It wasn't playing both sides of the fence—it was betting against yourself but still playing to win—and it encapsulated everything absurd and paradoxical that I loved about the French.

Manon and I thanked Danton, and his assistant appeared and hustled us back into the public area of the museum and into a glass elevator. The elevator offered a view onto the nave, and we saw a cleaning crew guiding power buffers across the floor below, swirling away scuff marks between the priceless bronze figures reclining on marble pedestals. A phalanx of black-suited men with briefcases appeared from the western entrance of the museum and marched purposefully across the nave. Our elevator reached the main floor in time for us to exit and trot around the corner before the officials arrived to press the Up button. As they bottle-necked through the doors of the elevator, we hid beneath a massive Hercules the Archer statue and waited until the elevator had carried them up to the administrative suite. Then we hustled out the main entrance, and Danton's assistant quickly swung the door closed behind us with a harsh metallic clack.

It was now pitch dark outside, and the densely falling snow turned the sky into a swirling black and white checkerboard. Manon dug a flimsy pink scarf out of her pocket and wrapped it around her neck. A centimeter of snow had accumulated on the statuary in the Orsay's plaza, and the tourists had all retired for the evening. We were alone.

"Our next move?" I said.

Manon shrugged. "L-L-Les Frigos." Her breath crystallized in a cloud between us and then drifted up into the night.

7

LES FRIGOS

By the time we met again at the Happy Elephant, Séverine had changed into a skintight white silk faille catsuit accented with a wide sash of shiny purple satin. She wore a matching purple satin head-wrap, and she had twisted fresh plant stems and leaves into her black curls—flat leaf parsley, chervil and arugula, among other salad fixings—turning her hair into a messy vegetable patch of organic trimmings. Leave it to Séverine, I thought, to find fashion accessories at the supermarket. She had finished the outfit with a lemon yellow alligator-skin overcoat lined with white fox fur, and cinnamon-colored leather thigh boots. She could not have called more attention to herself if she had strapped a laser-lighted disco ball to her forehead, and Manon's jaw actually dropped open when she saw Séverine—as if Manon's whole face had developed a stutter. Séverine kissed both me and Manon on both cheeks, though for my kisses she placed her mouth close to my own and lingered a little longer than was merely friendly. I smelled the chervil in her hair.

Jean-Pierre stood behind the bar, watching us with a twinkle of doom in his eyes. Funky syncopated jazz was thumping from the speakers behind him. He had opened the Happy Elephant this evening, as usual, not wanting to call untoward attention to himself by closing his bar on an otherwise ordinary Thursday evening, but the only customers on this snowy night were a group of Japanese tourists huddled together in the back, scrolling through pictures in the view-panel of a digital camera.

"I take it you'll be staying here, then," I said to Jean-Pierre.

"I'm no good in hostage rescues," said Jean-Pierre. "I'm slow and I run out of breath easily. I'll be home base, and I'll call the police if you get into any trouble. Besides, someone will have to bail you out, if you all get arrested."

Manon was the only one among us who had actually been to Les Frigos before, so she gave us a briefing about what to expect. There were two parts, she said, to the giant warehouse that had been converted from a cold-storage depot into artist lofts. Tiny theater spaces and galleries occupied the majority of the space, but at one end, accessible only through a separate outside entrance, was a popular jazz club, so there would undoubtedly be people around—artists in their lairs and jazz club patrons, at the least—so they would probably not meet their mysterious brick-thrower alone, strictly speaking. However, Manon said, the grounds of Les Frigos were expansive, with many hidden nooks and dark corners, and the warehouse was in a run-down, rough section of Paris, where unemployed immigrants mixed with unsavory bohemian types—drug addicts and opportunists—so it was not completely safe there. In fact, to most Parisians, the artists who inhabited Les Frigos were themselves unsavory types, tending toward the graffiti end of modern art, the naked-video end of filmmaking and the formless acid jazz end of modern music.

"Keep your eyes open," Manon said, "and watch your back."

We were at a decided disadvantage for a hostage swap, since we had neither the hostage nor the ransom, meaning that we would be pawns somehow—but a pawn can still capture the king, I told myself. Someone had called Jacques Martin wanting to meet tonight with the painting, so either this Third Man actually would bring the painting for reasons of his own, or we would all be his stooges.

We decided that Manon should drive her two-seater Z8 coupe to the jazz club, and that Séverine and I would approach the main entrance to the artist lofts on foot, from the metro. We all carried cell phones set to vibrate, with each other's numbers on speed dial, and we arranged to arrive independently at Les Frigos at 11:45pm.

I said, "Manon, you drive out toward Père Lachaise first, then around the peripherique to the thirteenth. If you see any-one following you, try to lose them. Séverine and I will head up to the Place de la République and change metro lines three or four times, to make sure we aren't followed."

"Don't do anything foolish," Jean-Pierre said. "Remember, the goal tonight is to rescue Benoît and stay out of trouble." He reached beneath the cash register and set two metal canisters on the bar. They were white cylinders with red push buttons on top and little cones on the sides, like tiny stereo speakers. "Air horns. They're surprisingly loud, so you can use them to find each other if you get in trouble, or just to scare people and buy some time. And don't be shy about using your cell phones. I'll keep my land line free."

Manon took one of the air horns, and I took the other. We clinked them, in a toast. Jean-Pierre rolled his eyes.

"Remember," said Jean-Pierre, "you don't know who you're dealing with, and they've already proven that they can be violent. If no one calls me by 12:30am, I'm calling the police."

"All right," I said. "We'll be careful." I shook Jean-Pierre's hand and fixed him a meaningful look.

"*Bon courage!*" he said.

* * * * *

We trooped outside, and Manon slid down into her

car, grave and excited, and drove off toward the Bastille roundabout, fishtailing a little on the snow-frosted street. Séverine and I headed toward the Place de la République, half a kilometer away, in the opposite direction from Les Frigos. The snow was drifting down in big, steady flakes that were collecting in earnest on the cars parked along the avenue.

At first, we walked in silence. I remembered the time I had covered the Abkhazia War in the early 1990s, and I had gone with a band of Georgian soldiers to meet some Abkhazian separatists at a train depot in the dead of winter, ostensibly to exchange hostages. The encounter had turned into a firefight that had left the snow around the depot crimson, but somehow the exchange had been made and both the Georgians and the Abkhazians left with their own soldiers restored to their ranks—at least, the ones who hadn't been shot. I didn't feel the sheer terror now that I had felt before that unfortunate encounter, as Séverine and I walked up the wide, quiet Boulevard Beaumarchais, but I reminded myself that Jacques Martin was a desperate, distraught man, that his helpers had managed to subdue Benoît and could probably do the same to Séverine and me, and that *The Despair of Pierrot* was potentially worth several million euros, a sum that could persuade people to behave irrationally. Martin would undoubtedly bring his henchmen, and a troop of undercover goons from the BRB might show up looking to incarcerate us. I didn't exactly expect a pitched battle, and no matter how crazy Jacques Martin might be, he was no machine-gun-toting Third World secessionist; but with this many people involved and this many unknown elements, I prepared myself for the worst.

I watched Séverine walk in her white catsuit, the bottom hem of her yellow alligator coat swinging in graceful arcs. She seemed committed to playing a part out of a Hitchcock thriller, as a kind of homage to our extinguished love. I feared that she wanted a taste of danger just to show me that she was a dangerous woman.

"I know what you're thinking," she said. "But love is not a competition. I'm not trying to win your love back."

"Then why are you out here tonight?"

"I've known you for more than ten years now, Luke, and I've always worried about you, whenever you go off to cover some war. I've always wished you would choose a safer way to make a living. But there's something about this whole affair that makes me wonder if my choices have, in fact, been too safe, that maybe I've been missing something."

"Missing something how?"

"Giselle goes to Africa with you, doesn't she?"

"Giselle helps the Red Cross hand out rice. She doesn't go into combat."

"I just mean," Séverine said, "that maybe I should have taken more risks in my life and maybe I would have understood more about myself, if I had. More about you."

Séverine was one of the most daring people I had ever met, within her own milieu—she had risked her life's savings to start her *chapellerie*, and she risked her reputation and livelihood every season with her designs and inventions. Séverine's risks, however, were not life-and-death, and she performed feats of derring-do only within the rarefied hothouse of runways and fashion shows.

"Séverine, risking your life over some obscure Expressionist painting isn't going to teach you anything about yourself that you don't already know. Risking your life is easy. Losing people you care about is hard. That's the real risk."

Séverine thought about that for half a block, watching the toes of her own boots scuff snow from the sidewalk. "Did you ever love me, Luke?" she finally said. "Is that why it was so easy to leave me, because you never really loved me?"

I recalled the slideshow of James Ensor's work that Manon and I had just seen at the Orsay, and Ensor's obsession with masks. All the carnival characters in Ensor's paintings hid their private sorrows behind festive disguises—Séverine, in her extraordinarily colorful, risqué outfit, could have stepped directly off the street and into one of Ensor's disturbing canvases, emotional mask and all.

"I still love you, Séverine."

She stopped and stared unblinking down the avenue. "Don't say that, Luke, don't just toss it off like that." Her cheeks flushed rosy from the cold.

"It's the truth. But it doesn't mean that you and I should be together. You said yourself just a moment ago that you don't want to win me back."

"Yes, but I lied."

Snowflakes landed in Séverine's absurdly coiffed hair. Her lemony coat seemed to shine pale sunshine into the wintry night. She finally turned to look into my eyes, and in them I saw the enveloping warmth of her hopes and her needs. I kissed her forehead.

"This is not the kind of conversation you should have right before committing a crime," I said. She nuzzled her face inside the collar of my pea coat and squeezed my waist. Her breath warmed my neck.

I thought of Manon's assertion that I was risking her relationship with Giselle by trifling with Séverine; if nothing else, I was risking my relationship with Giselle, and I marveled at how I was allowing it to continue. I wondered what need I had left unfulfilled in my relationship with Séverine that could be so compelling now. "Come on," I said. "We can talk about this later, if we still think there's anything to talk about. We have more pressing concerns."

We broke our embrace and hurried toward the République metro stop. I sensed that Séverine walked with a lighter step now, that she seemed altogether more spry after our brief cuddle and the promise of more talk of these things to come.

* * * * *

Séverine and I traced an insane spiderweb through the metro lines, taking the number nine from Place de la République, the seven to Gare de l'Est, the four all the way north to Montmarte, the twelve back across the Seine to Saint-Germain, the ten out toward the Eiffel Tower and finally the six to Chevaleret in the thirteenth. Once, as we changed trains at Gare de l'Est, I thought I spotted the man who had followed me from Séverine's shop to Giselle's apartment. We were descending the stairs onto the number four platform, and the horn sounded, warning that the train was about to leave. We dashed for the car and just slipped in before the doors slammed shut. The train pulled away, and our mysterious follower ran up behind, too late. Just before our car entered the tunnel, I glimpsed him swearing at his shoes in disgust, but I never quite convinced myself that he actually was the same man, and I thought that, if he were an undercover officer from the police or the BRB, he wouldn't have lost us so easily. And, anyway, those organizations have radios and cell phones.

Only one other person exited the metro with us at the Chevaleret stop—an old Chinese man—so I felt confident that, for the moment at least, we were not being shadowed. The train rumbled by overhead. Chevaleret was one of the few stations where the Underground went above ground for a short distance, and we hurried along in the deep darkness beneath the elevated train tracks.

The thirteenth arrondissement had a dubious reputation:

it was a depressed industrial *quartier*, known equally for its shipping yards and its "Chinatown" (whose residents were actually from all over Southeast Asia). The ugly modern apartments there, some as many as thirty stories high, had been built hastily in the 1960s to accommodate a flood of new immigrants, and they catered to poor people, who crammed whole families into tiny living spaces and scraped by however they could, legally or not. Tonight, except for a few dodgy stragglers in threadbare coats rushing by on questionable errands, we were alone. The street was eerily quiet.

The stark, geometrical apartments along the boulevard to our right shared none of the medieval charm of the Marais. They were giant concrete rectangles with thick iron balcony rails, which looked like prison bars in the midnight shadows. The building facades were decorated like giant bathroom stalls, with square tiles arranged in patterns that attempted to be whimsical but instead became grotesque parodies of whimsy, like an office birthday party. On the ground floors of many of the high rises were shops, but unlike the little boutiques and specialty markets in the older buildings downtown, these tended to be convenience stores or tacky Chinese restaurants that smelled rancid from half a block away, lit by turquoise and pink neon beer signs.

Soon, the buildings gave way to an abandoned freight train switching yard on our left, and a block later, the blank dark shapes of the *Bibliotheque Nationale de France* loomed across the railroad tracks. The BNF was a campus of four steel and glass buildings constructed in the shapes of giant open books, set among the urban blight of disused warehouses along the Seine. It had been one of Francois Mitterand's many attempts to add public buildings with novel architectural concepts to blighted industrial areas, and it meant that we must be close to Les Frigos.

I checked my watch—twenty-five minutes to midnight, right on time. I dialed Manon's number and learned that she was already parked in the Les Frigos lot, sitting in her car outside the jazz club. "B-be prepared," she said. "It's like a c-carnival here." We hurried up the rue de Tolbiac, which was as quiet and dark as the rest of the neighborhood; as soon as we rounded a corner toward the Seine, however, Les Frigos emerged out of the darkness, and it was clear that a massive party was underway.

Huge red and yellow spotlights swept across the face of the warehouse: the lights turned the snowflakes the colors of hell. Artwork completely obscured Les Frigos' outer walls, which, from two blocks away, seemed crude but had a certain chaotic charm. Two third-story windows had become the eyes of a giant spray-painted silver bumblebee, and one window on the fifth floor was now the mouth of a snaking Chinese dragon. Much of the spray paint, though, was merely graffiti, which formed hornets' nests of incomprehensible words sprayed over words sprayed onto words, in every color imaginable, and not one square centimeter was free of paint. As we approached, the fast, rhythmic thrum of techno music began to echo off of the walls around us, and when we passed a vast metal shed and came to the open parking lot of Les Frigos, we found it full of cars and people, and the music suddenly boomed loud—the soundtrack of heart attack. A poster at the gate declared that we had come to a *"post-post-post-moderne théâtre spectacle de l'esprit de l'homme."*

Some college-aged punks with spiked hair and heavy army jackets were loitering against the corrugated metal fence that surrounded the compound, and they took one look at the greenery in Séverine's hair and offered her the joint they were smoking. When she declined, they offered her a swig from a bottle of something orange, and we walked past them, through a gate into the parking lot.

As we approached, it became clear that Les Frigos had seen better days. Beneath the graffiti, it was a fairly typical, square shipping warehouse, whose heavy stucco had chipped off in great patches to expose crumbling brick beneath. A dilapidated grain elevator on one side had had its modest charm obliterated by graffiti, and on the railroad side, farthest away from the Seine, a semi-detached white square tower with an incongruous black tile roof stood guarding the train tracks leading into the compound. This tower was striking for being completely free of graffiti, its blank walls like a new canvas, and for having Normandy windows, as if a Picard chateau had been transported whole from the coast of La Manche. It was a stylistic rummage sale.

We wended our way between cars in the parking lot, most of which mirrored the building in both their dilapidation and "artistic" paint jobs. A swarm of people buzzed around the main entrance, and it occurred to me that it was going to be difficult to find any particular person in this crazy crowd. I scanned the mob for any signs of a conservatively dressed seventy-year-old mushroom but saw no Jacques Martin. The faces were all much younger, slathered with hideous face paint, topped with fantastically swirling or spiked hair of every imaginable color, each design more outrageous than the last.

At the building's main entrance, an especially tall, especially stoned, especially black man wearing a metallic gray unitard and sporting enormous sideburns dyed sky blue opened the door for us. "Enjoy the show," he said, in Nigerian-inflected English. The wide entry hall almost made me vomit: like the outside walls, every free space was obscured by graffiti, including the floor and ceiling, and the effect was noxious, claustrophobic and disorienting. The acid-house music and smell of old urine multiplied the effect: it was like swallowing your own head and finding yourself inside-out in your bowels.

Doorways opened on either side of the hall, and inside the dimly lit rooms crowds were milling around kinetic sculptures. Canvases hung on the walls, floor to ceiling, though even these gallery walls were graffitied, so it was sometimes difficult to tell where a painting ended and the wall began. Below the level of the music, a kind of industrial hum of shouted conversation garbled my mind. It was an experience of complete surreality, of sensory overload, until the boundaries between the noise in my own mind and the chaos all around seemed to disappear. Everyone we saw seemed to be tripping on some kind of hallucinogen, which must surely have beautified the otherwise painful ugliness.

At the end of the main hall, a metal spiral staircase led up into the center of the warehouse. Séverine looked at me for guidance. I nodded yes, and we ascended to the second floor. At the landing, four large metal doors with metal levers, like the doors to walk-in refrigerators in restaurants, led in four different directions. We chose the nearest one, pulled it open and went in. We found ourselves at the back of a forty-seat theater—every seat was filled, and the denizens were staring intently at a black and white film projected by a noisy sixteen-millimeter projector. The film was an American "race film," a movie made by blacks in the Jim Crow south in the 1930s or '40s, featuring all black actors, with apparently no budget whatsoever, judging by the sets and lighting. It was a gangster film, and a couple of guys dressed as Sicilian Mafiosi were threatening two other guys dressed as businessmen. The theater reeked of marijuana.

"If you guys don't pay us now," one of the Mafiosi said, "you'll pay later."

"And not just with money," said the other.

Someone in the audience hissed. I motioned for Séverine

to retreat to the landing, and we closed the door behind us.

She looked at her watch. It was already five till midnight. "How are we ever going to find them?"

I looked from one meat locker door to the next. Apparently, the city had forgotten to install heat in the building when they had converted it to artist lofts—the building still felt refrigerated, which may have been why it retained the name Les Frigos. It seemed colder inside even than out, despite the humid press of people all around.

I motioned for Séverine to try the next door. To get to it, we had to fight our way past a young couple dressed in identical Frankenstein masks, who intentionally interfered with us as they came up the stairs. I body-checked the man into the metal stair rail. Séverine pulled open the door and we went in.

Someone screamed, "*Fermez la porte*," and we slammed the door shut behind us. Unlike the cramped movie theater that we had just left, we found ourselves now in a spacious, open, almost empty hall with pure black walls and a clean floor and ceiling—a great relief after the riot of shapes and splattered colors. We seemed to have left the chaos of Les Frigos altogether for the kind of modernist gallery you might find in Saint-Germain, and the framed canvases on the wall reflected the more staid sensibility of the artist: though not academic or formal, the paintings were representational, using heavily applied oil paints in primary colors to depict quaint outdoor markets and bourgeois card games. At a table near us, glasses of champagne and canapés had been laid out on polished silver trays. I helped myself to a tart of smoked duck with chives, which was delicious, and washed it down with a sip of cava. Though the thumping techno bass-and-drums still pounded the walls here, we heard the strains of a Beethoven violin concerto competing against it. This gallery also had the benefit of some heat—we could no longer see our breath in front of our faces—and quite a few exit doors, partially concealed by heavy red curtains. At the very back, behind a partial wall, another metal staircase spiraled up into the darkness, and we seemed to be in a central showroom at the very heart of the warehouse.

Fewer than fifty people were milling through the gallery, and though they were dressed in carefully tattered punk garb, they stood before the paintings holding glasses of champagne, leaning into one another to comment on the works, exactly as if they were attending a black-tie event. A makeshift island had been created down the center of the gallery out of red velvet theater ropes, and within the ropes, sculptures stood awaiting our judgments. A group of people wrapped together in a king-sized coverlet shuffled from sculpture to sculpture in silence, their brows furled at the apparent profundity of the works. At the far end, another group had gathered around one of the displays and suddenly an excited festival of jabbering broke out.

I felt my phone vibrate, and I opened it to find a text message from Manon. "Two cops in blue turtlenecks hanging around jazz club." I showed it to Séverine, who gave me a worried look.

The group at the back of the gallery formed a wall of overcoats blocking the aisle, and we couldn't push our way through to the sculpture that was inspiring their discussion. "The fact that it's temporary doesn't mean it's not art," one man said. "Everything is temporary, including every work of art."

"Right," a woman said. "Think of Christo. Think of Buddhist sand paintings."

"I'm not saying it's not art because it's temporary," another woman said. "I'm saying it's not art because it doesn't fall within the realm of artistic content."

"Who are you to decide the content of art?" someone yelled.

"Intent matters as much as content," someone else said.

"Would you call a grenade explosion art?"

"Is the grenade intended to destroy something or make an artistic statement?"

"What if it's intended to do both?"

"What's the content of a grenade explosion? It has no content. It's performance art, at best."

"Are you saying that an act of war can't also be a work of art?"

"Yes, that's what I'm saying. For instance, in this work, the intent to take and hold a hostage falls outside the legitimate goals of art because it involves use without consent."

At the word "hostage," I pushed my way into the center of the group, and Séverine slithered through behind me.

"Who says there's no consent?"

"Even if there's consent, it's still not sculpture—it's performance art."

I elbowed a space for us in the unwilling mass of bodies, which reeked of reefer smoke and body odor.

"Are you talking Kant or Heidegger?" said a man with orange flames tattooed around his eyes. "Besides, this sculpture clearly has artistic aims."

"But it's not sculpture," said a ghostly pale woman wearing a false nose and horn-rimmed eyeglasses. "It involves embodying, not representing. I'm not sure it's art at all."

I looked past the tattooed man to the sculpture, and I found that I agreed with the woman wearing the false nose. It wasn't art, at all—it was Benoît, tied to a chair! He was unconscious, dressed in his usual green City of Paris coveralls. White twine rope had been wrapped around his ample midsection several times, his wrists were bound in front of him with a red bandana, and each of his legs was tied separately to the chair with green ribbons. Another red bandana had been stuffed into his mouth as a gag, and his head was lolling to one side. Beside his chair was a white placard, on which, written in hand, was the word *Otage*—Hostage!

"Why are you so devoted to categories?" said a bald man wearing an aluminum-foil headband.

"It matters what you call something," the false-nose woman said. "In order to have any understanding of the artist's intent, we have to know what the words we're using mean, and this simply isn't sculpture. It's performance art."

"What's your definition of sculpture, then?"

"Benoît!" Séverine cried. She shoved the debaters violently aside and stepped over the velvet ropes. "Benoît!" She touched his face.

"Hey, get away from there," aluminum headband said. "You can't touch the art!"

"This isn't art, this is my friend!"

"See!" false-nose said. "It isn't art."

"It's art because the artist says it's art! What about Duchamps' 'Bicycle Wheel,' or Warhol's soup cans?"

Séverine had removed Benoît's gag and was untying his hands. "This is an actual hostage!" she yelled.

"No, it isn't. It's labeled *Otage*! Nobody labels an actual hostage!"

"No, but they do call a hostage a hostage," said false-nose. "The category is all-important."

"Are you saying that someone labeled 'Hostage' can't be an actual hostage, at the same time that he's also a work of art?"

"You're kidding!" a drunken man in the back of the group said. "Just because someone's in an art gallery doesn't mean he's a work of art, whether he has a label on him or not. What if I slapped a sign on your back that read 'audience' and said you're a work of art? Would you be an audience member or a work of art?"

"What if I slapped a sign on your back that said jackass—would you be an actual jackass?"

I joined Séverine behind the theater ropes and freed Benoît's legs. A woman wearing a full pink ballerina skirt held up by men's suspenders was grabbing at my arms, trying to stop me from dismantling the 'sculpture.'

"Where's the artist?" false-nose said. "If anyone can clarify the intent here, it's the artist."

Everyone stretched their necks and scanned the gallery. My cell phone vibrated with another text from Manon. "Cops busting jazz club. I sneaked out to car. Get away?"

"There he is!" a man said, pointing back the way we had come.

I followed the man's finger toward the other end of the gallery, where an old, short, bald man in a black overcoat was busy unhooking a framed canvas from the wall. My heart raced.

"Jacques Martin!" I yelled.

The man whirled toward me and held his hands out in front of him, as if he expected to be attacked. When he saw that, in fact, no one was even near him, he snatched at the canvas in a panic and yanked it from the wall. As he turned, I saw the painting full on—it was none other than *The Despair of Pierrot*!

I jumped up and sprinted after him. He waddled none too spryly toward one of the side exits, and I caught him just as he put his hand on the doorknob. I grabbed a fistful of his coat collar and slung him around with all my strength. Martin clutched desperately at the painting as he came off of his feet. His shoes traced an arc through the air and he landed hard, twisting awkwardly onto his hip, flopping with a sickening thud onto his back. The corner of the frame smashed into the floor and cracked, and Martin lost his grip on the painting, which fell on its face.

I jumped over the old man and pounced on the painting. As I grabbed hold of the cracked frame, I turned to see the little cluster of amateur art critics huddled around Benoît staring at me, their eyes as big as ping pong balls. I was holding *The Despair of Pierrot*. But what could I do with it? The police were downstairs at the jazz club, and I was already wanted for stealing it!

I stood paralyzed, until Martin kicked my shin, and my left leg turned into a cold glass bottle of pain. I cried out and kicked the old man square in the chest, flattening him to the floor. I jumped up and ran toward the side exit.

Séverine was now standing next to Benoît, unsure whether to stay with him or follow me, and the punk philosophers clustered around her were watching the scene unfold as if it were a modern morality play. "Stay with Benoît!" I yelled. "The cops are on their way!"

A shot rang out! I heard the whistle at my ear and the ricochet across the room before I saw the chunk missing from the doorframe next to me. I flung the door open and slipped through, as skinny as I could make myself. Another shot! As I ran into the corridor, I glanced back and confirmed that Martin was lying on the ground shooting a revolver. A third shot hit the door as it closed behind me.

I found myself in a narrow stairwell lit solely by a spinning red light. The floor was a steel grid, and a steel grid staircase led up—but not down! I felt as though I had entered a Dada diorama, where all the absurdities were real. An old man with a gun was shooting at me, I was holding a stolen painting worth two million euros, the cops were busting people at the jazz club on the ground floor, and my only way out was up.

I ran up the steps two at a time. My left shin nearly gave out every time I pushed off of it—the spot where Jacques

Martin had kicked me felt like an empty hole, without strength or substance. I passed the third floor. At every landing another red light spun around and around, like the emergency lights atop an old police sedan. On the fourth floor landing, I was forced to jump over three people writhing together in some kind of post-modern sexual trinity, and I landed awkwardly and slammed my shoulder into the cold metal wall. I was desperately out of breath.

On the fifth story landing, I unintentionally smacked the corner of the frame against the railing, which sent stingers up my elbow. In the dim red light, the frame seemed badly split, and I tried to wrench it apart, to free the canvas—to no avail. I was stuck with the unwieldy mass of it. Another gunshot blasted from the stairwell below. I flung open the landing's metal meat locker door and wrestled the painting through.

I found myself in a room ten meters square, lit by candles. Three black steel candelabras hung from the ceiling, and an array of stools and tables stood along the walls, each of which held as many candles as could possibly fit. White wax had dripped over all the edges, into congealed pools on the floor. The air was suffocatingly still, the candles burning all the oxygen away, and at first I struggled to make out what the mass in the center of the room was, until I realized that it was twenty or so people sitting cross-legged in a circle. They were all wearing black monks' scapulas with hoods. Invisibly mounted spotlights cast cool yellow light on what seemed, at first, to be huge canvases of religious art on the walls—giant modern reproductions of medieval pietas, Last Suppers and Noah's Arks—but after a moment's examination, it became clear that all of these seemingly Biblical scenes were actually composed of pornographic photo-mosaics. Each giant religious picture was made up of small photographs, variously tinted to achieve the shades required to make the larger devotional compositions make sense, yet each tiny picture was a photograph of a bizarre sexual act. The music here was deafening, the drum-and-bass pounding a syncopated effrontery that only cocaine might calm.

I took the scene in all at once, in a flash, while desperately searching for an exit, but, except for the one I had come through there seemed to be no doors at all in this gallery, nor even a window. It was as if the pornographic monks had sealed themselves into a dead end. Suddenly, as if on cue, all the monks' hoods turned toward me at once. The hoods themselves were so deep that I couldn't see any faces inside. It was nightmarish. They stood up en masse, and I spun around, ready to face Jacques Martin's gun in the stairwell instead. That's when I finally saw the door next to the stairwell. As I turned to run, I felt a draft of fresh air coming from underneath it. I flung it open, ran through and nearly crashed into a row of filthy sinks. A public restroom!

I slammed the door shut behind me. No lock! At the far end, a row of toilet stalls guarded rectangular windows up near the ceiling—one of the windows was cranked open, and I scrambled into the stall, jumped up on the toilet seat and peered out into the night. For a moment, I couldn't find my bearings—the night outside was all swirling snow and weird industrial shapes. I finally found the dark line of the Seine, and then the sloping roof below me coalesced into the top of the jazz club. I had traversed the entire length of Les Frigos and stood staring down at the opposite side of the warehouse. At the side of the club, a police car's blue and red lights were strobing silently, turning the white snowflakes as they passed before it into a Pop Art representation of France's national flag. Directly below my window, I detected figures moving in the shadows, an exodus of people slinking through the winter darkness away from the police.

I heard scuffling outside the bathroom door. I dug the cell phone out of my pocket and dialed Manon, who picked up immediately.

"I have *The Despair of Pierrot*," I said. "I'm in Les Frigos, above the jazz club. I'm dropping the painting out of a window behind the club. I'm hanging up and then dropping my phone with the painting. Do you understand? Hang up, go behind the jazz club, dial my number and follow the sound of the ringing to the painting."

"*D'accord!*" I heard as I cradled my phone in the palm of my hand and then lifted the painting awkwardly, using the fingertips of both hands. The cracked frame stuck splinters into my fingers as I slid it out the window. I took a deep breath and let everything go.

The phone separated immediately from the canvas and plunged like a stone straight down into the night. At first, the canvas fell straight, too, but near the third floor a gust of wind caught it and wafted it out toward the parking lot and then back again, to and fro, floating it flat on the breeze like a maple leaf; then it dipped sideways and spun down like a helicopter blade, knifing into a snow bank, among a chaos of snow-covered shapes lit dimly by reflected light from the parking lot.

I had only a moment more to silently wish Manon luck and hope my cell phone survived the fall. The bathroom door burst open. I whirled and jumped off the toilet, ready for demonic monks or a pistol-wielding Jacques Martin; instead, a burly blond man in a blue police jumpsuit screamed at me to get down on the floor. He held a nine-millimeter pistol aggressively in front of him and sighted me in. I showed him my empty hands, and he screamed at me again to get down on the floor. Unfortunately, he was blocking me in, and there was no room in the bathroom stall for me to drop, so I remained crouching awkwardly, trying to kneel between the toilet and the half-open stall door, showing the cop my palms. He was all adrenalin and hostility, and he banged the stall door open, slamming it wickedly into my shoulder. His face turned red, and sweat streamed down his Neanderthal brow.

"Get down!" he yelled again, as if that might make it more possible.

"I can't." In order to comply with his order, I would have to take a step out of the stall.

He re-gripped his gun alarmingly. I took a step forward, trying to shoulder the door open and lower my eyes submissively at the same time. The cop's full weight slammed into me, and I lurched back. My feet slipped out from under me on the slimy floor. The last thing I remember was the cop flailing comically above my head. His gun flew out of his grip toward the toilet. The back of my head hit porcelain, and the thrumming nightmare of techno music abruptly stopped.

8

In Defiance of Nudity

When I regained consciousness, I was escorted roughly out of Les Frigos in handcuffs and set out in the snow by my burly blonde attacker, where I waited for the police paddywaggon to arrive, along with a host of other vandals and troublemakers. Among the artists, stoned hippies, pickpockets and jazz cats manacled to themselves and each other, I saw no one who seemed to have the wherewithal to steal *The Despair of Pierrot* from the Grand Palais or the motive to bring it to Les Frigos. Benoît looked particularly down at the mouth and had trouble even forming words. Jacques Martin could speak but wouldn't.

I was chauffeured to Les Halles Police Station for the second time in twenty-four hours, my head throbbing and my shin swelling. I wondered where Manon was, if she had managed to get away with the canvas.

* * * * *

At the station, I met the same officer who had banged on my apartment door the previous evening and taken Séverine's statement after the brick-throwing incident at her shop. He truly seemed never to sleep. He watched, self-satisfied and contemptuous, as I was led away to a holding cell.

"I knew we would catch you eventually, Monsieur Johnson, but after a single day? We're ahead of schedule."

"What have you caught me doing, exactly?"

Séverine, Benoît, Jacques Martin and I were processed

and questioned, along with a whole cadre of Les Frigos habitués, including a woman improbably named Ludivine Brindejonc de la Colombe de la Crochais d'Oilliamson—the artist in whose show Benoît had been displayed. Ludivine Brindejonc de la Colombe de la Crochais d'Oilliamson was an outcast from an ancient royal Anglo/French family, and her dodgy personal history was even more complicated than her name, including many arrests for drug possession and public disturbances. When Séverine and I had been in her gallery untying Benoît, Ludivine Brindejonc de la Colombe de la Crochais d'Oilliamson had been smoking kif with another artist on an upper floor of Les Frigos, and by the time she came back to her own show, giggling uproariously from the effects of the Moroccan marijuana, the police had already twisted Jacques Martin into a pretzel. Ludivine Brindejonc de la Colombe de la Crochais d'Oilliamson had found Martin's struggle extraordinarily funny, so funny that she had begun applauding the policemen for their fine work and shouting, "Encore!" For the requested encore, they twisted Ludivine Brindejonc de la Colombe de la Crochais d'Oilliamson into a pretzel, as well, which gave the artist a new perspective on their original performance. By the time she was sitting next to me in handcuffs in the paddywaggon, heading for Les Halles, she was in tears, and the kif probably made the whole evening seem much more tragic than it actually was.

The police questioned me separately for more than three hours, using many tried and true tactics—good cop, bad cop; threats; relationship building chitchat, including the sharing of gum; periods of calm followed by violent outbursts; false revelations of confessions made by my comrades; and so on. In fact, they asked a lot of questions that I would have liked the answers to myself, though I found it downright weird that *The Despair of Pierrot* had found its way into and out of Les Frigos without the police seeming to notice—none of their questions led me to believe that they even guessed it had been there: it was as if the kidnapping of Benoît and Jacques Martin's crazy shooting spree had had nothing at all to do with the stolen painting.

So what had the police been doing there, I wondered. They had known to conduct a raid at Les Frigos on the evening that the stolen Ensor showed up there, but the calculus of this equation became more mysterious as they questioned me. If they had heard Jacques Martin's message on Giselle's answering machine, they would have known that Martin had been there to swap his hostage for the stolen painting, but they did not question me about that, even though I was one of the prime suspects in the theft of the canvas from the Grand Palais. They understood that there must be some connection between the theft, Séverine's shop window and the shootings at Les Frigos (which luckily injured no one), but they seemed not to be connecting the dots. Yet, they had sent enough men out to close down the entire post-post-post-modern spectacle and arrest half the attendees.

More mysterious: someone had brought the painting to the galleries but had left without it. Martin hadn't brought it, though he had known which gallery it would be hanging in: how had he known? Who had put it there? Did Martin think that Giselle had put it there? Who had called him, impersonating Giselle, to arrange the swap in the first place?

Stranger still: how had Benoît been turned into a sculpture and when? Was Jacques Martin collaborating with Ludivine Brindejonc de la Colombe de la Crochais d'Oilliamson? Had her gallery been selected at random for the exchange or was she being paid to participate? Had Ludivine Brindejonc de la Colombe de la Crochais d'Oilliamson even known that the person who had stolen *The Despair of Pierrot* had hung it in her exhibit? Surely, a struggling modern artist—even an extremely stoned one—would know better than to display the most famous stolen painting in France in her own show. Had the artist herself stolen the painting and then displayed it, as a performance art piece? If so, had she also thrown the brick through Séverine's shop window?

* * * * *

The main problem for the police in this case was producing any evidence at all against most of us. Ludivine Brindejonc de la Colombe de la Crochais d'Oilliamson claimed to know nothing about any of it and said she had never seen Benoît before the police had arrived; however, even under the sometimes bizarre Napoleonic Civil Code, claiming ignorance does not excuse you from holding a hostage in your own gallery, no matter whether he was a sculpture or not, and the police held her for complicity in Benoît's kidnapping. Benoît swore out a long, involved statement against Martin; and, in addition to Benoît's grievances against him, quite a few witnesses had seen Martin shoot at me, so he was held for a list of crimes whose gravity was undeniable: kidnapping, assault with a deadly weapon, attempted homicide, criminal mischief (a category that could have applied to anyone there that night, I thought, including some of the police) and various somewhat random misdemeanors, including unpaid parking tickets dating back almost a year.

Those same witnesses who had seen Martin shoot at me had also seen me take a painting out of the gallery, though no one identified it as the Ensor, and I claimed to have dropped it in the stairwell, having taken it in the first place (so I claimed) merely to provide myself cover against Martin's pistol shots. No painting was found in the stairwell, of course, but I also had no painting with me; and since Ludivine Brindejonc de la Colombe de la Crochais d'Oilliamson showed no interest in prosecuting me, and since a painting in her gallery would ostensibly belong to her, the question became moot. Since it is not yet a crime in France to be standing on a toilet when a policeman bursts into a public restroom, there was no evidence of any particular crime for which to hold me. Jacques Martin did me a favor in this regard: even though he knew that I had taken *The Despair of Pierrot* away from him, he said nothing, since doing so would have implicated him in the theft in the first place, compounding his troubles. Moreover, I believed that Jacques Martin would rather have seen his precious James Ensor go missing than be returned to Pierre Bergé. Fortunately for everyone but the police, the attendees of Les Frigos who might have seen *Pierrot* hanging on the wall had been either too stoned or too guilty or too ignorant of its extraordinary importance at that moment to call anyone's attention to it, and I wondered how long it had been hanging on the wall before Martin snatched it. All evening? Five minutes?

Séverine, in a rhetorical move of surprising cheek, claimed that I had invited her to go to Les Frigos for the "art happening," and that she was essentially an innocent bystander. She said that she had been enjoying the debate about the meaning of art when a fight had broken out, and that was all she knew about it.

"You're an innocent bystander?" the officer in charge of my case said to her, as we were leaving the police station. "Your shop was vandalized this afternoon while you were speaking to a suspected art thief." He motioned toward me. "Then you attend an 'art happening' in the company of this suspected art thief and, while there, you happen upon a kidnapping victim, who, strangely enough, is a personal acquaintance of yours? And instead of being alarmed, you become involved in a debate about whether or not your friend is a work of sculpture? Surely, you don't want me to believe that you are merely an innocent bystander?"

"I certainly didn't throw a brick through my own window," Séverine said indignantly. "So I have no idea what you might be implying by that accusation." Her ire somehow seemed all the more real because of the vegetation now wilting in her hair. "And I didn't kidnap my friend Benoît. Are you accusing me of that? Are you saying I'm a kidnapper? Are you saying I'm an art thief?" Her performance impressed me.

By four in the morning, Séverine and I had both been released. Giselle remained, bafflingly, behind bars, though that was the Napoleonic Code for you! We had lost contact with Benoît, but he was at least safe in the well-heated Les Halles Police Station when we left, which was a huge relief.

And still no one had heard from Manon. It was unclear if the police even knew she had been at Les Frigos.

* * * * *

Séverine and I walked down rue Beaubourg in a daze. After the commotion and the stress, the silent streets seemed surreal, but welcoming. It was the hour after late-night revelers tottered home and before the bakers and fishmongers got up, and more than an inch of snow had gauzed the avenues and sidewalks, absorbing every sound. The snow continued to fall, now in exhausted, featherlight flurries, making the night's silence visible. In my twelve years of living in Paris, this was my first glimpse of a snowfall heavy enough to round the rough edges of buildings and bicycles parked on the street, snow so milky it was blue, snow like a ripped fringe of sky laid quietly over steeples and gargoyles and rusting cars, snow unsullied by the tumult of traffic and a million hurrying footsteps and urinating dogs. Despite my aching head and shin, despite my labyrinthine thoughts leading only deeper into themselves, I stopped for a moment and breathed in a deep cold draft of air and felt the tips of my ears turning numb. The snowflakes that clung to Séverine's coiffure for a few seconds before melting into the wilted salad of her hair seemed magical.

"I guess there's no chance of a clean getaway," I said, nodding at our clear footprints in the snow.

"Anyone who wants to find us knows where to look, anyway."

"Do you still have your cell phone?" I said. "Let's call Manon." Séverine took out her phone. "Better yet, why don't you call me, instead? Let's see if I answer."

She dialed my cell number. We waited until my recorded voice answered. "Shall I leave you a message?"

I closed the phone in her hand, thoughtlessly, meaning only to answer her question with a gesture instead of a word; but I found that we were now standing still on the avenue, two figures holding hands, facing one another in our own private snow globe. An unmistakably sexual look entered Séverine's eyes. Our breath mingled before us, and she leaned into me with her whole body.

Her phone vibrated between our hands, and my heart jumped. She held it up to look at the digital display. "It's you!" she said. I grabbed the phone and answered it, "*Allo! C'est de la part de qui?*"

We both heard Manon's voice. "Is it okay to t-t-talk?"

"*Oui, oui.*"

"You just called me?"

"We just called!" Séverine said. "What happened?"

"Do you have it?" I said.

"Have what?" Manon said. But the tone of her voice was triumphant.

"Are you somewhere safe?"

"N-not n-n-necessarily. Maybe we should s-stop speaking on your phone."

"Okay, but you're all right?"

"For the m-moment. I'm fine."

I gave Séverine a great bear hug that lifted her off the ground. When I put her down, I was already taking energetic strides down the street.

"Luke!" Séverine called. "What does it mean?"

I still had not had a chance to tell Séverine what I had done with the canvas after I had fled Ludivine Brindejonc de la Colombe de la Crochais d'Oilliamson's gallery. I whispered excitedly. "It means we have the painting! We have *The Despair of Pierrot*."

"And what does that mean?"

My feeling of triumph crashed into tiny shards on the street. What *did* it mean? It meant that Manon now had the painting that her mother was in jail for stealing, that half the police in Paris were looking for.

"It means we have problem."

I stared up into the swirly white night. Séverine hooked her arm through mine once again and guided me down the street.

"*Allons-y*," she said. "You'll walk me home and tell me all about it."

Séverine touched my cheek with her fingertip. We had downtown Paris all to ourselves, our own private winter wonderland. The snow had transformed all of the signs and fixtures and window ledges along this usually busy street into a vast, animated Impressionist painting, with streetlamps throwing yellow pools of light onto the snow. Séverine caught a straggling snowflake on her tongue and smiled at me, seemingly quite happy about her deepening involvement in the most high-profile art theft in France.

* * * * *

By the time we arrived at Île Saint-Louis, I was exhausted, not least from trudging through the deepening, wet, beautiful, irritating snow. The metro had not started running for the day, and I was nearly asleep on my feet. Séverine invited me up to her apartment.

"I'll sleep on the day-bed," I said.

"Suit yourself."

Île Saint-Louis is the most expensive real estate in all of Europe. Séverine's family had owned her four-room flat there for seven generations; otherwise, even on a couture designer's relatively extravagant salary, she could never have afforded it. She did earn enough to furnish and decorate it impeccably, and the interior reflected Séverine's sensibility: classic flair, with antiques, leather furniture and Persian rugs covering beautifully refinished hardwood floors. She had also included a few outré decorating elements—like the life-sized peacock spreading its wings opposite her bed, and the copper honeycomb sculpture, complete with copper bees, pupae and pollen, affixed to the entire length of one bathroom wall. I flung myself down on the day-bed in the living room, while Séverine went into the bathroom.

"I'm going to be a few minutes," she said. "I have to separate these greens from my hair. Would you fix us a drink?"

"A drink?" I tunneled into the throw pillows.

"I'd like my bedtime story with a bit of liquor. It's not every day someone shoots at me."

"They didn't shoot at you, they shot at me."

"Fine. Keep the romance for yourself. But it's still not every day I lie to the police." She turned on the water in the bathroom sink and shouted above it. "I kept some of that fancy armagnac you liked so much, from Isabelle."

"Not the Di Montalcino?"

"*C'est ça.*"

"But that was more than three years ago!" One of Séverine's best clients had given her a bottle of 1904 Di Montalcino as a thank-you gift, and the experience of tasting it had made me affirm everything I had ever done in my life to bring me to that moment. "Why do you even have a single drop of that left?"

"Because I'm not a lush like you."

My leg was killing me where Jacques Martin had kicked it, and I pulled my pant leg up to look at the bruise. Deep purple. I went into the kitchen and opened Séverine's liquor cabinet.

Séverine's armagnac was right where I had last seen it, and the level of liquid in the bottle had hardly changed—still nearly half full. Not being a lush was one thing—not enjoying a rare bottle of hundred-year-old brandy called a person's entire value system into question. I found two glasses and poured, at first lightly, respecting the liquor's rarity, and then with a heavier hand, honoring its fineness, feeling the contradictory impulses of French socialism at work on my American soul. The ancient amber liquid was complex just to look at and seemed to change hue with each tilt of the bottle. I re-corked it, held my glass up to my nose and inhaled the sweet, floral scent. I took a sip and tasted orange and oak, and it became intensely honeyed as I swallowed. A feeling of well-being spread through my body.

I carried our drinks back into the living room and felt a pleasant déjà vu. From Séverine's living room window, you could see one edge of a flying buttress holding up Notre Dame Cathedral, across a channel of the Seine, on Île de la Cite. I sat back down on the day-bed.

My thoughts were soupy. I certainly could not ask Manon

to walk into police headquarters with the stolen Ensor and try to explain what had happened. For one thing, I didn't even know what had happened, really, didn't know how the painting had found its way to Les Frigos and into our hands. If we turned it over to the cops now, the BRB would throw us in jail.

I held my armagnac up to the light. At two million euros for the painting, I could buy fifteen hundred bottles of this rare hooch, provided that so many bottles even existed still. If you drank only a sixteenth of a bottle a day, that would be enough to last more than 50 years. It might be worth the risk.

The water in the bathroom had stopped running. "Are you all right?" I said. I stood up and took a step toward the hall. "Séverine?"

Séverine stepped into the bathroom doorway. She was drying her wet hair with a yellow hand towel, and she was completely naked. "I'm fine," she said.

She posed for a moment with her head cocked slightly to the side and her hip jutting out on the other side, so that her body formed a long, graceful curve. Her years in the fashion industry hadn't been wasted! Even the exact framing she had chosen for her pose seemed perfectly calculated to enhance her beauty: she stood off center in the doorway, so that the curve of the bathtub behind her left hip flattered the slope of her waist, and the straight line of the side jamb emphasized the swell of her breast. She leaned slightly, letting the weight of her breast fall out toward her armpit, adding yet another curve to her figure. She stood that way only a moment, an artist's model, before she walked with aplomb to the day-bed, as if it should seem perfectly natural for her to be naked.

I knew every inch of Séverine's body already, but the surprise of seeing her naked flesh, and the ease with which she displayed herself were startling. And, once again, I noticed her perfume—she must have just applied a new scent. She had never used colognes or perfumes when we had been a couple, and this relatively insignificant change implied other changes, perhaps more dramatic ones. The scent she had chosen to wear now was like an appetizer at a Christmas party, with red pepper and cloves and some sweet earthiness underneath.

She threw her hand towel back into the bathroom, where it landed in a heap—also a very un-Séverine-like gesture—and she swirled her armagnac under her nose. "I should tell you, Luke, that I didn't really enjoy the stress and danger of this evening." She drank, then closed her eyes as she swallowed. "It was crazy. I was crazy for going there." She shook her head. "And poor Benoît tied to a chair and gagged! I felt so bad for him. And I thought you were going to be killed." She touched my arm. "Right in front of me." She drank again, a long deep, appreciative swallow, then set her glass on the end table behind her. "Does it make you uncomfortable that I'm naked?" She sat down and patted the cushion next to her. "Sit," she said.

My biggest concern at that moment was that we were ruining our enjoyment of the Di Montalcino. In defiance of Séverine's nudity, I took another long, appreciative drink, and let the honeyed ginger linger on my tongue until it burned. I sat down. Séverine moved closer, until her bare hip pressed against mine.

"We're not going to make love," I said.

"Yes, we are." She caressed my cheek and kissed my neck below my right ear.

"Look, Séverine, I'm not sorry that I kissed you in your shop, but it was a moment of weakness. Truly. We're not going to make love."

"You came up to my apartment! And anyway, this isn't about what you want. This is about what I want." Now she took my armagnac and drank from it. "In our whole relationship, Luke, we always did what you wanted. Even the way our relationship

109

ended was your choice. For me, there was nothing about our affair that wasn't somehow a compromise that I made for you, because I wanted to be with you so badly. And you? You were with me whenever you felt like it, and not with me whenever you didn't feel like it. You went off to Montenegro or Chechnya or Pakistan and risked your life, with no concern about how that affected me at all."

"Earlier tonight, you said you had always been curious about my life, about the risks I had taken. You said you wished you had taken more risks."

"I was wrong." She curled her legs up under her and leaned back into the pillows. "To have actual bullets ricocheting past your head! I don't know how you can face gunfire over and over again—and not just a wild shot from some nervous old man like Jacques Martin, but real gunfire from trained soldiers." She scoffed and drank. "It's absurd. I should have broken up with you many years ago. It was horrible being with you, Luke. Every time you left Paris, I died a little inside, and yet you left again and again. You left me so many times!" She snuffled a little and fought back a tear and then drained the rest of my armagnac in one go. "And then you just left me for Giselle all of a sudden. If you knew how much I suffered! And how much I've been in love with you still these last two years, in spite of it all."

"I'm not sure I understand."

She shrugged. "What's unclear?"

"You're angry at me. You're bitter against Giselle. You say you should have ended our relationship many years ago. But now you want to make love with me?"

"We're going to make love because I want to, whether you understand why I want to or not."

I took a deep breath and nearly fell asleep, but Séverine kissed my eyebrows and I rose back to consciousness. Sleep seemed like a daydream of a memory of a vision of an idea of a hallucination I had once had in my youth. "Look, Séverine, my head is like a garage with too many cars parked in it. A man tried to kill me tonight, and I'm wanted by the police for a crime that it now seems I might actually have committed, albeit somewhat differently than they think. Really, this is the worst idea in the world. Would you hand me your glass of armagnac, please?"

She obliged, and I drank again. Séverine took my free hand and placed it on her breast. Her nipple was hard, and she inhaled deeply, so that the soft mass of her flesh moved in my palm.

"But you're not obliged to be faithful to Giselle if you're not married, Luke. It's just a convention." She took the glass from me and drained this brandy off as well. "Anyway, you weren't faithful to me. Maybe you're not the faithful type." She set the second empty glass next to the first one and began unbuttoning my shirt. "You're going to make love with me because this is how we're going to make things right between us."

I shook my head no. "How will this make things right?"

"You're going to cheat on Giselle with me, just like you cheated on me with her. And for the rest of our lives, whenever I look at her, I'm going to know that you weren't faithful to her, either, and you're going to know it, too."

Ah, I finally understood: revenge sex.

"It's not complicated, Luke." She stood up on her knees on the day-bed and put her breasts right in my face. "How many times have we made love? Thousands of times! This is just one more time among thousands. And when we're done, we can all be friends again, just like the old days."

"Except that Giselle and I will still be together," I told her left nipple.

"I don't want to be with you any more, not as your lover,

not as your wife," Séverine said. "Tonight, I just want you to be unfaithful to Giselle. She doesn't even have to know. I'll know."

"Manon will know."

"How?"

"She'll just know."

"Well, I won't tell anyone." She ran her fingers through her own hair, impatiently combing out the tangles.

"And Eugene?"

"I won't tell him, either."

She bent forward to kiss me, and I pulled away. Séverine wanted me to be the kind of person who cheated, so my cheating on her would not seem so personal. She wanted to look at me holding hands with Giselle and know that I was a liar, and think that, when I had left her for Giselle, I had done her a favor. And she wanted one last time with me, so that the last moment of our sexual relationship was the one she chose, not the one I had imposed on her.

I didn't think that what Séverine wanted was unreasonable—only unethical and perhaps immoral and emotionally unbalanced. "Look, Séverine, I'm not going to make love with you. *Tout à fait sérieusement.*"

She held her breath a moment, and then slid down into my arms and lay half across me. "Really?"

"It's better not to. Really. For both of us."

"Will you at least sleep with me in my bed? Just for the comfort of it, if nothing else? Please."

"All right. On one condition."

"What?"

"Put something on."

Is it adulterous to sleep in the same bed with your ex-lover while your current lover is in jail? Giselle might have thought so, if she had walked in and seen us snuggled into one another under Séverine's comforter. Then again, being French, she might not have. I imagined that Eugene would not have thought highly of the arrangement, nor would Manon; but then, they were French, too, so I could not be sure. Perhaps they would have congratulated us on our restraint.

9

NAPOLEON LE TIGRE

I slept like a dead planet for a couple of hours and then awoke in an orbit of panic. I had no idea where I was, what day it was, what was happening. Even when I finally recognized Séverine asleep beside me, I couldn't figure out what she was doing there.

I ached all over, and even the dim morning light felt like hot lava pouring into my eyes. I looked at Séverine's sable curls tumbling loose across her face, her mouth open, her deep breaths approaching snores. I tried lying back down next to Séverine, but this felt all wrong, and I grew more and more tense. I couldn't stay here.

I got up and tiptoed into the bathroom. The hot shower felt good, and I tried to let the splashing water tell me where I should go next. Call Manon? But if I went to see her, I would probably just lead the cops to the painting. Jean-Pierre? What I really needed was information.

First, I needed to know how *The Despair of Pierrot* had arrived at Les Frigos last night, who had put it there and why. Second, I needed to know exactly why the police had shown up—had they followed one of us there? If so, which one of us? Jacques Martin? Or had they followed the painting there, and if so, why had they not arrested the person who had delivered it? No, they seemed not to know that the painting had been there at all. Had someone tipped them off about Benoît after he had already been installed in Ludivine Brindejonc de la Colombe de la Crochais d'Oilliamson's gallery? If so, who had tipped them off?

I realized I should just do the same thing I always did when I had more questions than answers and didn't know where else to turn: call Jay Cutler. Jay was an old crony of mine who worked at the *International Herald Tribune*. He had been the Chicago *Tribune*'s man in Paris for many years while I was working for the New York *Times*, and we had often swapped stories over shots of Glenfiddich at L'Arbuci. After he had accepted an editorial position with the *Herald*, he had become something of an insider in the byzantine world of Parisian politics, and he had a shrewd understanding of Parisian society. He and his staff would be following the story of the stolen Ensor closely, and if any journalist had inside information about the Grand Palais or the police investigation, it would be Jay. I got dressed in my stale-smelling clothes from the night before, found Séverine's cell phone and dialed Jay's number.

A woman answered and told me that he was in an editorial meeting. Would I like to leave a message?

"Tell him Luke Johnson will be there in less than an hour, and that I know where the stolen painting is."

I decided to take Séverine's phone with me and scribbled a note telling her where I was going; and then, as I turned to leave the apartment, I remembered a pepperbox pistol that I had given her once as a souvenir of the Guatemalan Civil War. I had found it in a hardware shop in Guatemala City—the owner swore that William Walker himself had left it behind in 1859—and I'd spent my last quetzal on it before leaving the country. It was a revolver that fit in the palm of your hand, with a beautifully inlaid wooden handle and a three-inch revolving steel barrel, which had weathered to a fine light blue. Séverine had found it charmingly tiny and hung it on her living room wall as a decoration—a four-shot .32 caliber pistol that was most useful to her as a knick-knack. Of course, I had never bothered to find bullets for it, but I slipped the pepperbox into my outer pocket anyway and left for Jay's office.

* * * * *

The *International Herald Tribune* was headquartered in the west-Paris suburb of Neuilly-sur-Seine, out toward the skyscraper business community of La Defense, where the most giant of France's international companies had their headquarters. It was a straight shot to La Defense down the number one metro, so I made the short walk from Séverine's apartment to the Hôtel de Ville station. The brisk winter air helped clear my head, and the slow, bewildered traffic, honking and swerving and mounding dirty slush into the gutters, somehow made me feel more at ease. The overnight snow had created an atmosphere of shared difficulty, a kind of holiday of disgruntlement, and people gave each other rueful grins as they slipped and slid on the icy sidewalks.

I stopped at a café for an espresso and stood at the bar, gazing watchfully at the gray day, but I spotted no one who seemed to be following me. I got on the metro. All the way out to Neuilly, the businesswoman sitting next to me texted an endless series of notes in the incomprehensible shorthand of stock market abbreviations.

The Herald Building was a slate-faced five-story structure on rue des Graviers that looked more like a sci-fi pillbox than the headquarters of a major European newspaper. I had spent a lot of time in this building when I'd worked for the New York *Times* (the Times Company owned the *Herald Tribune*) and I always felt a little mulchy and nostalgic when I came back. I loped up the steps, through the main doors and past the three-foot-tall bronze owl that welcomes visitors to the lobby. The receptionist greeted me with a familiar, "Hey, Luke, how ya doing," in her Milwaukee accent, and we made small talk about the snow while I waited for the elevator.

Upstairs, Jay's French receptionist, Clémence, raised her eyebrows. "*Ça roule?*"

"I always look this way first thing in the morning."

Clémence was a conservative mother of three from a small town in the Dordogne, and she took great pleasure in disapproving of everything at the *Herald*. "Go on in," she said. "Jay will love to see you in this condition."

Jay was scribbling in his notebook and puffing away furiously on his pipe, a blatant violation of the recent anti-smoking laws. His office smelled ashen, fetid and cherry-sweet, like a Danish dockside bar. He was wearing his customary Levi's jeans, long-sleeved Levi's denim shirt and a suit vest, and his gray hair was slicked back with too much brilliantine. He had expanded some around the middle since I had seen him last.

"Why is it I only see you *after* I print your name in the paper these days?" he said.

"You tell me—you're the one who prints it."

"Enough chat. Tell me where the stolen painting is and how you got mixed up in it."

"I will, but first I'm wondering if I could pick your brain about something."

"You mean *someone*, right? Pierre Bergé?"

Jay was always two steps ahead of me. "You'd make a good cop." I sat down in the leatherette chair across from him.

"Maybe you should have asked me about Bergé before you broke into the Grand Palais, and I could have saved you a lot of trouble." Jay tamped his pipe lightly with his thumb and then puffed it back to life. "What do you want to know?"

"First of all, I didn't steal the painting."

"But you know where it is? Or is that just a story you told Clémence so I'd cancel my meeting?"

"No, I know where it is. I'll tell you all about it, but right now I'm in a jam. I was at an 'art happening' at Les Frigos last night—you know, that bohemian flop house in the thirteenth?"

"You were there? We're working on that story now for our North American edition, but your name hasn't come up yet." Jay puffed a billow of dense gray smoke between us. "So that dust-up was about the stolen Ensor?"

"It was *all* about the stolen Ensor. Why, what angle are you covering?"

"Police raided the jazz club for hashish, and a gunfight spilled over into the art galleries. That's all anybody's saying."

"No, that's a cover-up. The shots were because of the Ensor painting. Look, I can't speak on the record, and you have to keep me out of this."

"Okay. We'll do a little quid pro quo."

"All right. Go."

Jay said, "If you have a hunch that Pierre Bergé is connected to Les Frigos, you're right. Bergé practically owns the place. Well, not any more, but he's the reason the city didn't demolish it twenty years ago, and he still supports it behind the scenes."

"Financially?"

"Financially, politically, every way that matters. He's their patron saint."

"Was he behind the student demonstrations that supposedly saved the place? I remember all the protests and sit-ins."

Jay laughed. "That was all socialist claptrap. I mean, don't get me wrong, the demonstrations happened and all: everybody loves to wave placards, but you know as well as I do that if there's no money, there's no socialism. Bergé essentially paid off the city to allow those artists to keep squatting there. The artists are socialists, but Les Frigos is a personal capitalist enterprise of Pierre Bergé. The protests and students—that was just something the papers hooked their copy on."

"Why did he do it? Is there money in it?"

"Bergé was in love with one of the artists."

"Ah, so it's not money or socialist claptrap that makes the world go round, after all—it's love!"

"Well, it's sex, anyway. Bergé endowed a fund to support artists and musicians through Les Frigos, but he didn't want to be associated with it publicly because he liked the atmosphere there, and he was afraid that, if his name became associated with it, it would become just another sex hangout for the fashionistas that hung around Yves Saint Laurent. He wanted it to remain a sex hangout for struggling artists. He manipulates everything to his own advantage, see, and Les Frigos is just too miscellaneous for him to manage, too random to be able to control as a brand. It would be a huge headache. So he just gives them money under the table through a fund that someone operates for him and then he lifts an artist out of the muck once in a while, when it suits him. For him, Les Frigos is a kind of minor leagues of art, and if someone he likes comes along, he takes them out of there and gives them their own show at a respectable gallery."

"And why did he get involved in the first place? Who was he in love with?"

"An artist who went by the name of Napoleon le Tigre."

Napoleon le Tigre, I thought. Séverine had told me that Pierre Bergé had been asking about Napoleon le Tigre before I had arrived at her hat shop, the day before.

"His real name was Vieau or Vichot," Jay continued. "Something like that."

"How about Vicaut? Benoît Vicaut, maybe?"

"Maybe. You know him?"

I told Jay everything I could about Benoît as quickly as possible: that he was an unemployed garbage collector, that he had been kidnapped by Jacques Martin in an ill-conceived extortion plot, and that he had been turned into a sculpture last night at Les Frigos.

Jay let out a low whistle and then puffed on his pipe. "A garbage collector, huh?"

"He doesn't actually have a job."

"I figured he'd died of AIDS or something way back when. I mean, what I'm telling you about Bergé and Les Frigos happened a long time ago. I've got an archive guy looking into every angle we can think of on this Grand Palais heist, and Napoleon le Tigre doesn't leave a trace after 1983."

Jay told me that Bergé and Napoleon le Tigre had had an affair that caused a scandal for the Yves Saint Laurent camp in the early 1980s, but beyond a few names and the connection to Les Frigos, they had uncovered nothing else about it. "Just the usual fashion nonsense, you know? It's an insular world, in many ways, so your story about this kidnapping might be our smoking gun." He tapped his keyboard and motioned for me to look at his computer monitor. I stood up and leaned across his desk to see a picture of Bergé from approximately thirty years before, looking quite a lot younger and quite a lot drunker than I had seen him last, at a party, surrounded by muscular, shirtless men.

I looked hard at the photograph and found a half-obscured face in the corner that could have been a young Benoît, but it was too blurry to tell for sure. So Benoît had been an artist called Napoleon le Tigre? I wondered if it could be true, that the rotund guy in the green coveralls drinking up the Happy Elephant's liquor all these years had once been an artist and Bergé's boy-toy.

"It would explain a lot if the Benoît I know was Napoleon le Tigre. It's still not clear how Jacques Martin got involved, though, or who he is."

"A lot of people were on the periphery of the Yves Saint Laurent crew in those days," Jay said. "It was an orgy of Mandrax and narcissism." Mandrax was the European name for Quaaludes, a favorite recreational drug among fashion models. Check the eyes of the models on the next catwalk you see: that glassiness might be more than just self-involvement. "Any number of people could have had affairs with Saint Laurent or Bergé at the time," Jay said.

I was still trying to get my mind around the idea that Benoît the Garbage Collector had once been Napoleon le Tigre the Artist. "I guess this kind of makes sense, Jay. But it still doesn't explain who stole the painting from the Grand Palais."

"I thought *you* stole it!"

"Be serious."

"You really have that canvas?"

"Yep. I was a pawn in a ransom swap that went wrong. Now I have to get rid of it before the police find out I have it."

Jay put down his pipe, sat back in his chair and looked down his nose at me, a pose that made him seem almost avuncular. "Why don't you just turn it over to the police, if you didn't steal it?"

"At this point, it would be hard to explain how I have it, and since they think Giselle and I stole it in the first place, I would have to present some evidence that someone else stole it. Evidence I don't have. Otherwise, they'll call it Burglar's Remorse and throw me in the clink."

"Turn it over anonymously." Jay told me about a story the *Herald Tribune* had printed recently about an art theft in São Paolo that was still unsolved, in which masked burglars had taken two million dollars' worth of paintings and jewels from a private residence and then left them near a television station the next day. They had phoned the station anonymously to reveal where the treasures had been hidden.

"Why did they give it back?"

"Nobody knows."

"I suppose that makes the most sense: just leave the canvas in a stairwell somewhere and call the cops. I just wish I knew what the hell was going on. I mean, was someone out to get me? Or Giselle? Or Benoît? Or Bergé?"

"Maybe they just wanted the painting."

"No," I said. "That's the sticking point. Whoever stole the painting already had it in their possession before all of this nonsense started, before Jacques Martin made his extortion threats. Martin wanted it, that's true, but by the time he visited Giselle with the ransom demand, the painting had already gone missing from the Grand Palais—it's just that no one knew it yet, certainly not Martin. Whoever stole it set Martin up at Les Frigos last night, and it worked: now he's in jail! Somebody out there saw Martin coming, and I think he was trying to frame me for the theft and get me and Martin both thrown in the clink in one fell swoop—but he played his cards at Les Frigos badly, because now I have the painting and I'm still free. Problem is, he knows who I am, and I don't know who he is or what he really wants, and I can't do anything with the canvas."

Jay knocked ash out of his pipe into a swooping silver Nambé ashtray. "But if you turn over the painting anonymously, at least you don't have to worry about being thrown in jail, and that will probably get Giselle off the hook, as well." He reloaded and re-lit the pipe. "And you might want the police to help you on this one. Martin took a shot at you, after all, so I'm not so sure this other mystery person won't, too."

"True. I'm not interested in martyring myself for Yves Saint Laurent's art collection."

"It's not the art, trust me. Love of art does not cause old men to kidnap other old men and fire guns in art galleries."

"Maybe it's not love of art, then, but just plain love. Martin said he wanted the painting as a keepsake of Saint Laurent."

"A keepsake worth two million euros, don't forget. That kind of cash can buy a lot of love where I'm from."

"You don't have a romantic bone in your body, do you?"

"I can't afford one," Jay said. "You're not gonna tell me where that painting is, are you?"

"No."

"Or how it made its way out of the Grand Palais?"

"If I knew, I'd tell you," I said. I promised him a bottle of Glenfiddich, and we shook hands warmly.

"Seriously, Luke, just turn the painting over to the cops. Your curiosity about somebody else's thirty year old love triangle is not a good enough reason to get killed."

* * * * *

I stood on the street outside the Herald building for a long time, trying to digest the information Jay had just fed me. I thought his idea of turning over the painting to the police anonymously was the most reasonable thing I had heard yet; but I started to wonder how I might turn this situation to my advantage. After all, we had been dragged into this affair against our will at great personal risk, and for the first time we were ahead of the game: Manon had a masterpiece worth two million euros, and it did not seem unreasonable that we might be compensated somehow for our trouble, especially given Pierre Bergé's vast wealth. It seemed possible that we could just cut through the nonsense about everyone's motives, make a simple exchange, and everyone could get something of value—Bergé could have his painting back, we could get clear of the cops, and we could make a fast million or two in the bargain. But where was Manon?

I took out Séverine's cell phone and saw the red light flashing. She had a text message. It was from her boyfriend, Eugene: "*Sans tu, ma minette, je ne suis rien.*" A love text!

I was suddenly jealous of Eugene's relationship with Séverine and wanted to destroy it, so I could have her for myself—this despite the fact that I had rejected Séverine's advances in favor of Giselle. But now I wished, in spite of myself, that I were back in Séverine's bed, picking leafy greens out of her hair. How twisted the human heart can be!

I dialed Manon's number, and it rang until her voicemail answered. Nothing good came to mind: Manon in jail. Manon slumped over the wheel of her car. Manon at the bottom of the Seine. *Merde!* I dialed her again. Nothing.

I walked a little way up rue des Graviers to the Cemetery of Neuilly-sur-Seine. This tidy garden of stone crypts was laid out in geometric patterns across a whole city block, with tall hedges blocking the view of the surrounding suburb. I had often eaten lunch here while working for the *Times*. A frosting of snow now covered the graves, and the denuded flower bushes showed only thorns. The tombs were carved with homely sayings, mementos of a quieter, more bucolic time, before Neuilly had transformed into just another business-park suburb. It was a good place to go when you did not know what else to do.

The red light on Séverine's phone flashed again. Another text message from Eugene! It's funny how even a little physical intimacy with someone, even your old lover, can start to work on your heart. I remembered Séverine's back pressed into my chest last night, the smell of her neck. I dialed Séverine's home number. No answer.

Footprints in the snow showed that some early mourner, eager to get a head start on his daily melancholy, had already visited a grave. At the very center of the cemetery, a cherubic stone angel guarded a massive crypt containing a whole family of eighteenth century provincial royalty. I looked into the hollow eyes of the cherub.

I wondered if it might be possible to strike a deal with the police so that Giselle could go free in exchange for the painting. She might be released, anyway, if the painting turned up anonymously, or the cops might prosecute both of us out of spite, whether the painting turned up or not. Séverine's cell phone rang. The screen identified the caller as Séverine herself, dialing from her landline. At the same moment, I heard a crunch of footsteps in the snow behind me, and I turned to see that a man in a gray suit and black overcoat was approaching from the street. I answered the call, and said, "Séverine!" The man pulled a pistol from his overcoat and shook his head no. Séverine said, "Luke? Did you just call me?" I put my hands up over my head.

"Monsieur Johnson," the man said. As he advanced, I finally recognized him as the one who had followed me to Giselle's apartment, the one who had asked for directions when I'd confronted him.

"Are you the BRB?" I said.

"No, Monsieur Johnson. I have an invitation from Pierre Bergé. Please come with me."

The pistol in his hand was a SIG Sauer P226 with a silencer, a model I knew well from my time in Montenegro. The SIG Sauer was a state-of-the-art Swiss locked-breech center-fire autoloader with a fifteen-round magazine. Under the circumstances, I decided not to reach for the unloaded nineteenth-century pepperbox I was carrying in my coat pocket.

"Luke?" Séverine's voice piped through the phone. "Is something wrong? What's happening?" I dropped the phone into the snow.

The man was perfectly calm, as if his "invitation" were the

most normal thing in the world. He was handsome in a shiny male-model way, with hard-shellacked brown hair that twisted into a single premeditated curl over the rugged prow of his forehead. His overcoat was obviously not off-the-rack.

Behind him, on rue des Graviers, a black limousine rolled up and stopped at the cemetery gate. He bent down and put Séverine's cell phone into his coat pocket. "*Après vous*," he said, and I started walking. I got into the back seat of the car, and Bergé's gun-toting lieutenant slid in beside me. Another shiny, sleek male-model type sat behind the wheel, listening to a Pet Shop Boys song at extremely low volume.

Rue de Babylone

When I had first been assigned to cover the Chechen War for the New York *Times*, my editor gave me a booklet published by the U.S. State Department about how to survive a kidnapping. The booklet was chock full of useful tips—it said, for instance, that it's best to travel through unfamiliar territory in groups, because terrorists prefer not to confront large numbers of people all at once, and that you should limit your routes to wide open spaces, where you can easily see terrorists coming from a distance. It also advised that terrorists might be irritable, nervous and uncertain, so if you found yourself in close quarters with a terrorist, you should not surprise him with sudden movements. A few years later, I read a U.S. Forest Service pamphlet that gave the exact same advice for bears.

Pierre Bergé's henchmen drove me across the Seine toward Faubourg Saint-Germain. The gray stone buildings along the Left Bank were wrapped in a cellophane of snowy winter light, making them seem distant and fake. We passed the Hôtel de Matignon, a mansion built in the eighteenth century by Louis XIV, where the French prime minister now had his offices; and the Hôtel de La Vallière, where the Daughters of Charity had once grown fruit and vegetables for the poor and now foreign ambassadors strolled beneath the trees, negotiating trade deals with the French administration. The whole area had the surreal splendor that time lends the aesthetics of the dead. When we turned onto rue de Babylone, it became clear that we were heading for Yves Saint Laurent's apartment—the apartment that had once held most of the art now on display at the Grand Palais.

We pulled up to a pair of arched steel double doors set into a stone wall, and the chauffeur punched a button on the dashboard. The doors swung inward, and we drove into a private carriage yard. Across the open space, apple and pear trees thrust a web of bare branches. The paving stones had been swept clean of the previous evening's snow, and the limo rolled to a smooth stop behind a silver Bentley. We waited while the automatic gates shut the city out behind us, giving us time to finish listening to the Village People's "Go West," the chauffeur bobbing his head purposefully to the beat.

I slid out of the car, and Bergé's lieutenant followed, pistol at my kidneys. The chauffeur led us across the courtyard to a dark green wooden door with vertical black stripes, which looked like a watermelon standing on its end. Inside, we walked along a short, well-lighted hall to a cage elevator. My captors' colognes waged a silent war in my nose as we glided up.

The elevator opened into a vast room with glossy black painted walls inlaid with gold-leaf swirls. A dozen floor-length mirrors were mounted on the walls or set on massive wooden stands around the room, reflecting both the room and the reflections of the other mirrors, creating a funhouse of infinitely reverberating images of armchairs and divans and paintings at slightly off-kilter angles. The furniture's intentionally clashing colors—yellow, green and pink—made a spumoni of Italian leather.

Except for a carefully snaking walkway through the middle, every square centimeter of the room—floor, wall and ceiling—held frescoes, paintings, furnishings and sculptures. It was as if Bergé had crammed a whole wing of the Louvre into his parlor, a priceless nightmare of opulence. Through a doorway to my right, a sitting room offered similarly dense and expensive décor, and I could only guess how claustrophobic the atmosphere must have seemed before they'd moved the "extra" half a billion dollars' worth of art to the Grand Palais.

Standing in the center of this lavishness was Pierre Bergé. He had finally changed out of his blue leisure suit and now wore an elegant, conservative gray silk suit, a red tie with whimsical yellow polka dots, and a yellow pocket square.

"Would you like a coffee?" Bergé said.

"One sugar, whole milk," I said.

Bergé nodded to his chauffeur, who disappeared through a door behind me. "It is no secret, Monsieur Johnson, that I want my painting back. I know that you or your associates have it. I must insist that you return it to me, as the sensible thing for all of us."

"I don't have your painting. We've already been through this."

"You didn't have it yesterday. You do now. You acquired it at Les Frigos last night."

"How do you know?"

"I still have a few friends among the Monks of Onan," Bergé said. I remembered the eerie chanting acolytes on the top floor of Les Frigos, in their robes and hoods.

Bergé's lieutenant with the SIG Sauer stepped around me and walked up the little snaking aisle toward the center of the room, nearly toppling a marble faun on a pedestal as he passed. Bergé chastised him with a tsk-tsk, and the gunman looked genuinely chagrined. He kept his finger near the trigger, but I noticed that the hammer wasn't even cocked—in an opportune moment, this might afford me an extra second before he could get a shot off, and I tried to identify a likely escape route. The nearest window was more than four meters away, and I would have to fight through an army of *objets d'art* to reach it—and it would be an unpleasant plunge to the street, even if I did. It seemed that the only real option was the elevator, but in order to escape that way, I would have to hold Bergé and his men at bay while the door slowly opened and slowly closed. Plus, they might be able to shut off the electricity while I was descending, trapping me even more efficiently than I was trapped now. Escape, in other words, seemed unlikely.

Bergé said, "You can't sell the painting, and you can't hold it long enough for the uproar to die down, since the police will watch your every move until the canvas is recovered. Eventually, its location will be exposed, you will be imprisoned, and the painting will be returned to me anyway. You might as well save yourself the trouble and hand it over."

"And if I *still* tell you that I don't have the painting?"

"Mere audacity won't help you, Monsieur Johnson. Better to deal with me than the police. I can call them any time and tell them you have it, and then what will you do?"

"Well, I don't have it, so I won't do anything. And if I want a police escort, all I have to do is walk outside and flap my arms. They're not waiting for your call."

"I am trying to help you, Monsieur Johnson."

I nodded at Bergé's lieutenant's gun. "And just how are you doing that?"

"Frankly," Bergé said, "I prefer not to deal with the police. They are likely to botch the job, just as they botched it at Les Frigos. I would always prefer to deal directly with the merchant."

Merchant? I thought.

The chauffeur returned with a silver tray. On the tray were four coffees, a sugar bowl, a cream pitcher and a plate of *petits fours*. He came to me first, and I added milk and sugar to an espresso and selected a macaroon. I sipped and munched while the chauffeur served the others. The gunman accepted his black coffee ruefully, eyeing the pastries but unable to hold more than a cup and a pistol. Finally, the chauffeur took a coffee for himself, though he seemed unsure what to do with the tray, so he stood balancing it awkwardly in one hand while daintily tilting an espresso to his lips with the other.

"In any event," Bergé continued, munching a pistachio finger. "I will have to insist that your friends exchange the painting for you. Claude here," he nodded toward the chauffeur, "will call them and make the demand, and then deliver you when the time comes."

Jacques Martin had held Benoît hostage to force Giselle to get the painting from Bergé, and now Bergé was holding me hostage to force Manon to give the painting back to him. Next, I would have to kidnap Bergé to force Benoît to give the painting to Giselle. Eventually, we would all end up kidnapping each other and have to exchange one another for ourselves.

"This can't possibly work," I said. "You can't keep me hostage here. The police are monitoring you, too, and you're connected to me already, so all I have to do is stay missing for a few hours, and the police will come knocking at your door. No matter how cozy your relationship might be with the *gendarmerie*, they're not going to let you hold hostages in your apartment. And if I know you can't afford to hold me, then where is my incentive to give in to your demands?"

Bergé sipped his coffee and nodded. "But I'm not threatening to hold you hostage, Monsieur Johnson. I'm going to kill you if you don't return the painting."

"Aren't you going to have to kill me now, anyway?" I said. "To keep me from telling everyone what happened?"

"What would you tell? That you stole my painting, and I kidnapped you to get it back? Ridiculous! That story would put *you* in prison, not me. Anyway, the fact that you're here now does not prove that I kidnapped you; rather, it proves that you came here to make a ransom demand. There will be three witnesses who say so, and it's even possible that your death could be the result of a struggle that you initiated while you were threatening me. In fact, that outcome would save me the trouble of hiding your body. There is no way for you to win, Monsieur Johnson, but you may lose gracefully by giving me back the painting."

The chauffeur had finished his coffee and set his cup back on the tray, which he stood holding out in front of him. He seemed unsure whether to stay and wait for our empty cups or take the tray back into the kitchen. He held it out to Bergé's gunman, who finished his coffee and set his cup on it, still lustfully eyeing the tartlets.

"Give Claude your cell phone and tell him what number to dial."

"He already has my cell phone," I said. "It's in his pocket."

"Claude!" Bergé said.

"I don't have it," the chauffeur said. "Maurice has it." He gestured at the gunman with his silver tray.

The gunman lowered his pistol an inch while he reached into his pocket for the phone. I had only a moment's opening, and I took it!

I lunged at the chauffeur, flipped the tray up into his face and body-checked him into the gunman. We all staggered into the statuary. The chauffeur tripped and fell backwards, and I flailed through empty air. I landed hard with my elbow in his face, and the air was filled with clattering cups and pitchers. A blueberry tartlet bounced off my nose and rolled under a couch. Bergé was shouting incomprehensibly, and I lost track of the gunman. I heard shattering glass and the heavy thuds of priceless objects crashing to the floor.

The high-pitched whine of bullets through a silencer made my blood run cold. More glass broke across the room.

"No, Maurice," Bergé yelled.

I got to my knees. The chauffeur lay unconscious beneath me, his bloody nose sickeningly off center, and Bergé was on his knees to my left. Maurice had landed on his derrière against one of the floor-length mirrors—his legs lolled over an upturned footstool. His gun arm was wedged awkwardly against a fallen marble statue of Diana the Huntress, and he was aiming the pistol in my general direction. He squeezed off another round, and I felt air from the slug rush past my temple. I dived for cover behind a giant alabaster chess king. A shot ricocheted twice and then lodged in the chair behind Bergé.

"Stop it, Maurice," Bergé screamed. "Stop shooting!"

Maurice unwedged his arm and began struggling to his feet, so I leapt up and ran the few steps to Bergé and downed the old man with a forearm shiver to his jaw. He flopped backwards and let out a pitiable groan. I reached for my pepperbox and grabbed Bergé by the collar, clinched his head in the crook of my arm and held my ancient pistol to his cheek. Maurice waved his SIG Sauer wildly at me and Bergé.

"Don't shoot, Maurice, for God's sake," Bergé said.

"Drop the gun," I said.

"Drop it, Maurice," Bergé seconded.

Maurice let the gun fall. "Get away from it," I said. The gunman took a step backward and flopped, like a marionette whose strings had been cut. His body crashed back and his feet kicked into the air—he had tumbled over a black stone panther! His head hit a marble pedestal holding a sculpture of a male torso. The pedestal wobbled, and the sculpture teetered for a moment and fell. It landed on the gunman's right shoulder and bounced. Maurice screamed and curled into himself.

I pushed Bergé down violently and grabbed the SIG Sauer. Claude and Maurice lay in their own private heaps of priceless art, and Bergé slowly and mournfully got to his feet and surveyed the damage. Sculptures were toppled; mirrors broken; a lamp lay against a sofa, its glass shade shattered. Maurice continued to moan, clutching his shoulder.

On the surface, I seemed utterly in control; but even though I held my own hostages now, it seemed impossible to use them. I couldn't call the police, not while holding Bergé at gunpoint in Bergé's own house, and the fact that Manon now had his stolen painting looked very bad. It looked, in fact, as if I had stolen the painting in the first place, just as the police suspected, and now I had come to do Bergé even more mischief: Bergé was right!

"Is that a Sharps pepperbox?" Bergé said. I was still holding the pepperbox in my left hand and the SIG Sauer in my right. "What year was it made?"

"Eighteen fifty-nine, supposedly."

"Four-shot, correct? What a beautiful piece! A pity you can't get ammunition for it any more."

So that's how it is, I thought. I'm holding Bergé at gunpoint, his lieutenant is rolling on the ground with a broken arm or something, his chauffeur is unconscious, and he's appraising my antiques. He was fearless *and* shameless.

"All right, let's go," I said. "Get my cell phone." Bergé climbed over the wreckage and searched Maurice's pockets for the phone, while Maurice groaned and writhed. Bergé accidentally kicked his chauffeur's head as he tried to hand me the phone, and he fell forward, crashing down between the chauffeur's legs. Claude suddenly woke up, and the three of them moaned together in unison.

"Get up, Bergé." Bergé struggled to his feet. "You, Claude! Make sure Maurice is all right. Don't call an ambulance or the police till I'm gone! If I hear sirens, I'm going to kill your boss." Claude lifted his head, but then moaned again and lay back down.

I made Bergé punch the button to open the elevator doors. I followed him inside and kept both pistols pointed at his heart. Why I continued this masquerade with the unloaded pepperbox, I don't know. Bergé pressed *Rez de Chaussées*, and we descended. The ride to the ground floor seemed to take forever.

"The truth of the matter is that I knew," Bergé said, confessionally.

"Knew what?"

"That Yves had had an affair with Jacques Martin. But I had no idea that Yves had promised Martin that painting, of all things, and I didn't know they had been in touch with each other before Yves' death."

"So you believe Martin's story?"

"Yes. It seemed cruel of Yves to do that to me, to indulge this insipid affair right up until the day he died, even after we were formally married. But it would be just like him."

"I don't understand."

"Yes, I have always assumed that you don't understand," Bergé sneered. "How much do you want for the painting?"

"I understand it's worth two million."

"It was appraised by Van Weyenbergh at three million. At the Christie's auction, bidding would have started at two. Are you always this imprecise?"

"Remember that I am imprecisely holding a gun to your heart," I said. "Let's split the difference. Two and a half million."

We reached the ground floor, and the elevator door opened. I shoved Bergé out into the courtyard, and we walked into the frigid January air.

"Bring me the painting, and I'll wire transfer the money to your account," said Bergé. "Give me your account number."

Ha! I thought. If Bergé wired two and a half million euros

into my account, which usually held less than two thousand, the BRB would arrest me immediately. Now that I thought about it, I could imagine no way that Bergé could give me two and a half million euros outside of handing me cash, and it seemed unlikely that he could produce such a volume of paper before the police discovered Manon's whereabouts and locked us all up.

I slipped the pepperbox into my pocket. "Give me your cell phone," I said. He offered me Séverine's phone, and I said, "No, yours." He found his own cell phone in his jacket and handed it to me. I dialed Séverine's cell number, and when it rang, I exchanged the phones and saw that Séverine already had Bergé's mobile number listed as "Yves and Pierre." I put her phone back in my pocket. "I'll call you in two hours with instructions. Open the gate."

We walked across the *cour d'honneur* to the wall protecting us from rue de Babylone, and Bergé punched a button to open the steel carriage doors. They swung silently, slowly inward. I uncocked the SIG Sauer and slipped it into my inside pocket, fearful that Bergé would start screaming his head off. Instead, he stood calmly with me, watching the gates roll in, as if he were escorting me to the street after a pleasant party.

"Will you still auction the painting, once you have it back?" I said.

"Of course! Why would I want a nasty reminder that Yves had betrayed me? I just didn't want that swine Jacques Martin to have it."

II

L'ART ET LA MODE

I walked to the Hôtel de Cassini and found a free cab at the taxi stand. Every moment, I expected to hear police sirens, or at least an ambulance coming to help Bergé's broken-limbed lieutenant, but as the cab pulled away from the government offices, all seemed quite normal. Diplomats in expensive silk suits and camel-hair overcoats were walking toward their meetings, talking heatedly on cell phones, while their attachés in frumpy office fashions scuttled behind them, lugging over-sized briefcases freighted with arguments. A whisper of snow was in the air, the sky uncertain about the future.

I dialed Jean-Pierre at the Happy Elephant and was re-lieved to discover that he was, at that very instant, pouring a glass of wine for Benoît, who had just turned up. I told them to sit tight, and then I dialed Séverine's home number and told her that Benoît was waiting for us at the Elephant. Finally, as the taxi crossed the Seine on Pont Royal, I dialed Manon. She answered immediately.

"L-Luke, thank God!" she said. "I'm in t-trouble."

"Where are you? What's happening?"

"I'm in the sewer. I d-don't want to tell you wh-where. I had to abandon m-m-my car."

The Parisian sewer system was a vast network of catacomb-like tunnels far below the city streets. Some sections dated from the middle ages, and they were large enough to walk through standing up.

"Are you all right?"

"I've been b-better."

"Do you still have the painting?"

"Yes, b-but—" Her voice broke up, and the call dropped.

I dialed her number again, but this time the call went immediately to voicemail. I slumped into the back seat of the taxi, which smelled of rotting grapefruit, Agua Brava, and roasted chestnuts, all swirled together in a stew of old sweat. Manon was in trouble somewhere in the Paris sewers!

* * * * *

When I rushed into the Happy Elephant, I found Benoît sitting at the bar, wearing his green City of Paris coveralls. Given the fact that he had been a hostage for the last week or more, he didn't look bad, and the strain of captivity had not caused him to shed any excess weight from his rotund belly. In fact, he seemed to have *gained* a little weight. A glass of wine so red it was black sat on the bar in front of him, and Jean-Pierre was standing behind the bar drinking an espresso. Benoît didn't even get up to greet me—in fact, he was in midsentence when I walked in, and he just continued talking, acknowledging me only by raising his glass.

"—which is exactly the kind of behavior that got him into this mess in the first place," Benoît was saying. "And that's why he deserves everything he gets."

"Manon is in trouble!" I told them about my conversation with her a few minutes earlier. Jean-Pierre poured me an armagnac, and I sat down at the bar.

"How could she end up in the sewer?" Jean-Pierre said.

"Actually," Benoît said, "it's not a bad place to hide. Remember Jean Valjean?"

I dialed Manon's number again, but her voicemail picked up. Either she had no signal or she had turned her phone off.

Or worse. "How do you find someone in the sewers of Paris? There must be a thousand miles of them."

"Two thousand kilometers, to be more precise," Benoît said. "Every hash dealer and smuggler has a map." Benoît was fifty-one years old, but he gave the impression of gruff, youthful vitality, not least when he offered simultaneously literary and streetwise observations.

I slapped Benoît on the back and gave him a little squeeze around the shoulders. "It's good to have you back again."

The front door flew open and Séverine rushed in. "Benoît!" She ran to him, and he spun on his stool, so she could throw her arms around him. Benoît reveled in her kisses. Jean-Pierre poured her a glass of wine, a bartender to the bitter end.

Séverine was wearing what I can only describe as a fur helmet—its shape was like the leather American football helmets of the 1920s, even down to the earflaps, but it was crafted from sheared beaver, dyed orange. The rest of her ensemble seemed bland next to this siren headpiece—black leather coat over a tangerine-colored cashmere sweater and simple black jeans. The orange laces of her black suede boots perfectly matched the beaver hat. I felt an overwhelming urge to take her into my arms, to feel her body pressed against mine. Séverine turned from Benoît and kissed me on both cheeks, and I breathed in her skin and hair.

"Luke!" Séverine said. "What's happened? Why did you hang up on me?"

I told her first about Manon and then filled the entire group in on my escape from Pierre Bergé.

"What a snake!" Benoît grumbled.

Séverine caressed my cheek. "Are you all right, Luke? My God, how terrifying!"

"Bergé is obviously in earnest," I said, and I put his lieutenant's SIG Sauer on the bar for proof. "But we have an offer of two and a half million euros on the table."

"Yes, and no way to collect it," said Jean-Pierre. "And no way to trust Bergé, anyway."

"I haven't even told you the strangest part. I thought Benoît might want to tell us about Napoleon le Tigre himself."

Benoît's face seemed to shrivel into itself. It was like watching a time-lapse film of a plum drying into a prune, all of his features desiccating into a single spot of extraordinary hatred between his eyes.

"Who the hell is Napoleon le Tigre?" Jean-Pierre said. He motioned that we should all move to the back table, where we could sit facing one another, and he opened a bottle of Faugères.

I cast a worried glance at the front door, and Jean-Pierre immediately jumped up and locked it. We are all, I thought, adept at reading different kinds of signals, the signals that most closely correspond to our own fears and desires. Jean-Pierre wanted security, so he understood when anyone felt nervous or threatened. Benoît wanted respect, so he was intensely aware of subtle gestures of insolence or mockery. And Séverine? I couldn't tell if, at the moment, she wanted love or safety or revenge, or maybe all three—which would make her the most acutely sensitive of all.

"Well, Benoît?" I said. "Or shall I tell it?"

Benoît downed the rest of his wine and poured himself another glass. "You should really ask how Napoleon le Tigre knew Yves Saint Laurent," Benoît said. "That's the real question."

"Who the hell is Napoleon le Tigre?" said Jean-Pierre again.

"When I first met Yves Saint Laurent thirty-five years ago," Benoît began, refusing to answer the question directly, "I was a very different person."

"You weren't his garbage collector?" Séverine said.

"The times were different. Everything was different. I was different." Benoît held his wine up to the light, as if seeing his past through the magic looking-glass of the Faugères. "Yes!" he thundered. "I was Napoleon le Tigre!"

* * * * *

It all started, Benoît said, in 1976, when he was a naïve kid from the Atlantic port town of Saint-Nazaire. His father had been a crane operator on the docks, and Benoît had hated the shipyard. He had a cousin living in the Latin quarter of Paris, and Benoît convinced his family to let him go for a two-week visit one winter, when the shipyards were slow.

"I never went back," Benoît said. "My cousin was living in a flophouse near the Panthéon, and he had the kind of life I had always dreamed of."

Benoît's cousin was a hashish dealer, and he introduced Benoît to a group of young people who had one foot in the student protest culture and one foot in the art world—two groups that crossed easily into one another through drugs, politics and music. Some of his new friends remained forever on the periphery of both worlds, losing themselves in pills and needles; but some were pretty enough, witty enough, or talented enough to gain entrée into the inner circles of the high art world, which in turn was connected to other largely nocturnal worlds, the haute decadence of fashion designers, rock stars and models.

"I started painting because my cousin used to fool around with acrylics, just for fun. When you deal hash, you have a lot of time on your hands. He would get really high and try to paint straight lines in all the colors of the rainbow, and then he'd call it art. His paintings were horrible, so I thought, 'Well,

I can make horrible paintings, too,' so I took up his brush. But it turns out that I can actually make paint look like things."

Benoît's cousin's hash clients would marvel at Benoît's work, and word got around that this crazy self-taught Breton was living in the Latin quarter making amazing art. Soon, people began showing up at Benoît's apartment for more than just hashish.

"It started as a way to pass the time, but then before I knew it, I didn't want to do anything else," Benoît said. "I couldn't even think about anything else. One of my cousin's regulars worked at a gallery, and he offered to let me hang a couple of paintings, so I did."

Coincidentally, the gallery owner knew Pierre Bergé, and one of Benoît's paintings caught Bergé's eye. Before he could say abracadabra, Benoît found himself at a table at Le Sept with Bergé and Yves Saint Laurent, and they liked him.

"A lot of these clubs and galleries were very gay," Benoît said, "at a time when gay culture was still underground. Within that community, people were more open to each other than they are now, because there were only a few places where they felt they could be themselves. Mandrax and hash and cocaine were everywhere, too, so the whole scene had this unreality and intensity: being gay, being an artist, a designer, a model—it was all very 'us against the world.' Every day was life or death."

Bergé loved Benoît and his paintings, and he soon made Benoît into a personal project. "Collecting art and promoting artists was just what Bergé did to express himself," Benoît went on. "He had so much stress dealing with Yves' tantrums and drug addiction, and running an international fashion business isn't easy, so he had little side projects of his own just to keep his sanity. Napoleon le Tigre was that kind of thing. He promoted my art seriously, but he turned my persona into camp.

It was the price I paid for his help: he promoted my art, and I became an artwork of his."

Benoît finished his second glass of wine and poured another rather larger one.

"It suited my idea of myself as an artist, at the time, going to these parties where I'd be the main attraction with my paintings, but there'd also be a bondage show, and the whole thing might turn into an orgy. Every night was something decadent and extreme."

"But Napoleon le Tigre?" I said. "It sounds like the name of a television wrestler or a breakfast cereal mascot."

"They were different times."

"But what happened to him?"

"While I was Napoleon le Tigre, I met everyone in Bergé's little circle, Lagerfeld, David Bowie, Roland Barthes, all the supermodels and rich playboys, including Jacques Martin. Martin was a diplomat's son, and he had been all over the world, so he told interesting stories. He was rich. He was witty. He dressed like Oscar Wilde. That was how he gained admission to the inner circles, and how he stayed, by having money and making vicious little quips about people. He was unkind, but he embodied the two traits that French fashion designers care about most: wit and fear.

"Anyway, Martin and I had an affair. This was thirty years ago. It lasted for several years, actually. It was through Martin that I discovered I'm not really gay, but it was quite normal to have such affairs back then. We all had affairs with each other, all the designers and artists and models. Some were just flings, but some caused real problems, the way sleeping around will cause problems in any small group." He gave me and Séverine a knowing look. "Martin was sleeping with Yves, too, at the time, and Bergé used me to get information about Yves' affair with Martin. Bergé was extremely jealous. Eventually, I got sick of it, sick of the whole charade and the pretensions and the orgies and the drugs, and I told them all to go to hell. They don't take kindly to that sort of thing, so they cut me out. Napoleon le Tigre simply ceased to exist, like countless other momentary notions.

"I hadn't heard a word from any of them in thirty years, until last week, when Martin found me and invited me to a party. I decided to go for old times' sake, just to see. I didn't know that he wanted to extort Pierre Bergé, or that he had any bad intentions, but the party was just an excuse to jump me and take me hostage. I walked right into it."

Benoît suddenly shouted, "Martin knows nothing about art! Art should arise from the romance of philosophy, not the philosophy of romance. It should become a metaphysics of mystery. He doesn't deserve that painting! He doesn't even know what it means!"

Séverine said, "Is that why you ultimately gave up art and that whole life? Because they didn't understand?"

"I stopped showing my paintings because no one took them seriously. I became a camp show, nothing more than an amusement, and, like I said, I just got sick of it. When I got off drugs, the whole thing seemed ridiculous. So I went back to school, tested into the *École Nationale d'Éboueurs* and became a garbage collector. I started working on an art de vivre instead."

Séverine's cell phone rang in my pocket and I jumped. "Manon!" I said. But when I held it up, I found that it was Séverine's boyfriend Eugene, instead. "I need to answer this," she said. She snatched the phone from me and excused herself. The wave of anxiety I felt about Manon was nearly equaled by the wave of jealousy I now felt over Eugene, which splashed down into my stomach.

"I'm going to call the police now and tell them to find

Manon," Jean-Pierre said, angrily. "I don't care about how it all fits together any more! We can't leave her in the sewers!"

"She's probably running *from* the police, Jean-Pierre! We can't just lead them to her. She has the stolen painting!"

"But we have to do something."

I thought of Jean Valjean's adventures underground in *Les Miserables*. Valjean had used the vast network of tunnels under Paris to escape from Police Inspector Javert. "Paris has another Paris under herself," Hugo wrote. "A Paris of sewers, which has its streets, its crossings, its squares, its blind alleys, its arteries, and its circulation. Paris's great prodigality, its wonderful festival, its Beaujon folly, its orgy, its stream of gold from full hands, its pomp, its luxury, its magnificence—is its sewer system."

"We could arrange a rendezvous with Manon," Benoît said. "Some of the older buildings downtown have access directly into the tunnels, for maintenance. Printemps, for instance. We could leave Manon a message on her phone to go there, and we could get her out that way."

My thoughts were like artificial fog billowing across a stage production of *Les Miserables*. Benoît was suggesting we try to rescue Manon through the basement of the busiest high-end department store in Paris, Printemps!

Séverine returned from her phone call and sat down next to me. "Your story still isn't complete, Benoît," Séverine said. "I understand how you fell into Jacques Martin's trap on the barge and how he kidnapped you, but how did you wind up as a sculpture in Les Frigos?"

"That's the simplest part of the story," said Benoît. "Ludivine Brindejonc de la Colombe de la Crochais d'Oilliamson is Jacques Martin's illegitimate daughter."

"I thought Martin was gay," I said.

"He is gay! That doesn't mean he can't have sex with

women. You have a surprisingly simple view of sexuality, Luke."

"Please forgive me," I said. "I'm American."

Someone pounded on the Happy Elephant's door. We all turned in alarm. Waving in at us through the plate glass window was Giselle!

Jean-Pierre let out a delighted, "Hourra!" and rushed to let her in. My eyes met Séverine's, and my heart leaped into my throat.

12

HARLEQUIN APPEARS

Jean-Pierre bear-hugged Giselle, and Benoît and I attached ourselves to the two of them, forming an ungainly mass of human particles with Giselle as its nucleus. She eventually slithered wholly into my arms and kissed me on the lips, and then she noticed Séverine standing near the bar waiting to greet her. Séverine never came to the Happy Elephant any more, not since I had left her for Giselle, so her presence alone was odd, and her attitude as she approached us was also surprising: she opened her arms and strode forward, cat-like, one foot in front of the other, for an embrace and kisses on Giselle's cheeks.

"I'm so happy they let you go," Séverine said, uncharacteristically breathless.

"Séverine! Thank you." Giselle looked to Jean-Pierre and Benoît for some explanation for Séverine's presence. Jean-Pierre stroked his beard and smiled broadly, and Benoît shrugged and drank his wine. She turned to me, confused. Séverine still embraced her. "They said they didn't have enough evidence to hold me, but I think they just wanted to follow me. It's some kind of tactic."

"Yes, of course," I said. "Come have a glass of wine. We have a lot to tell you."

Jean-Pierre poured another glass of Faugères. "Where is Manon?" said Giselle. "I couldn't reach her."

"Let us tell you the whole story. She's fine, but the truth is we don't know exactly where she is. A lot has happened."

"You don't know where she is, but she's fine? Why shouldn't she be fine? What do you mean?"

Séverine finally released Giselle but then took her by the hand and led her to a table, and now I grasped her other hand, almost as if we were competing for her. Jean-Pierre pulled a chair out, and we still did not let go as she sat down, forcing Giselle into an awkward little lurch. Jean-Pierre stumbled out of the way, and the scene became downright weird. Giselle pulled her hands away, and I let go first, losing the contest to Séverine, a fact that Séverine emphasized with a triumphant preening look, though I did not understand exactly what we had been competing for. Giselle looked to me for an explanation, but Jean-Pierre chose that moment to raise his glass in a toast to Giselle's freedom.

Once again, we were obliged to recapitulate the whole story of *The Despair of Pierrot*, Giselle grasping at my hand and squeezing it harder and harder as the escapade unfolded. When we had finally brought her up to the moment, she sat back and stared at us all. She was grinning the kind of grin you see on accident victims, as they sit in the backs of ambulances next to their wrecked cars.

"Let me see if I understand," Giselle said. "Manon is in the sewers with the painting, the police are chasing her, and Pierre Bergé wants to give us two and a half million euros to get the painting back or he wants to kill us or both?"

"That's the size of it."

"Well, it's obvious," said Giselle. "Either Manon leaves the painting in the sewer and we pretend the whole thing never happened, or we risk handing it over to Bergé and take the money. What other choices are there? We can't go to the police now. They're just waiting for an excuse to arrest us again."

"The trouble is," I said. "Manon has dropped out of communication, so there's no way to know if she's safe, or if she's been caught, or by whom, or what. The only way to get messages to her is to leave them on her cell phone and hope she's able to receive them, and if someone has her, they'll receive the messages and know all of our plans instead. So as long as we don't hear from her, we won't be able to help her or plan anything or do anything. We're stuck."

"If Manon had been picked up by the police, she would have called us," Giselle said. "The thing to worry about is Bergé and his henchmen. If they're chasing her, that could be dangerous."

Benoît said, "The sewers worked for Jean Valjean! That's how he saved himself from being shot!"

"And Manon loves that book!" Giselle said. "She must have chosen the sewers deliberately."

"I hope that's true," I said. "But let's think about things we can actually control. I think we should call Bergé and accept his offer. We'll set a meeting, whether we intend to keep the appointment or not. At least, that will box him in. Then we can stop worrying about his men trolling the streets, because he'll be busy preparing to jump us at a ransom exchange. Anyway, I think we should actually ransom the painting back to him, if Manon still has it and we can manage to find her somehow."

"And when Bergé turns you over?" said Jean-Pierre. "Then the cops will have the evidence to convict all of us!"

"No," Séverine said. "If I know Bergé, he just wants his painting back. That's my opinion, anyway. He won't even miss the two and a half million—that's just a bad day at cards for him."

I said, "Bergé told me that he only wanted to make sure that Martin doesn't get the painting. His main concern in all of this, I think, is to avoid having a sordid scandal attached the auction. He wants to canonize Yves Saint Laurent with all of this charitable giving, and the last thing he needs is some jilted ex-lover stealing his paintings and making a lot of noise about Saint Laurent's affairs."

"But you and Giselle are still wanted for stealing the painting," Jean-Pierre objected. "The RMN will arrest you the minute they see a mysterious two and a half million show up in your bank account. They're not going to allow a break-in of the Grand Palais to go unpunished."

"Give Bergé my Swiss bank account," Giselle said. "The RMN can't touch it."

Giselle had kept a Swiss bank account for just such large, discreet transactions when she had run her family's antique business. Dealing in rare antiques from ancient family estates, she would routinely handle transfers of hundreds of thousands of euros. The Swiss wouldn't bat an eye at two and a half million, and they kept their transactions private.

"Of course, he may be setting us up for the cops, anyway," Benoît said.

"No," I said. "Anyone willing to kidnap me and hold me hostage won't be likely to go to the police. The bullet holes in his walls won't lie. I'm starting to like the way this sounds. We all have reasons to keep the cops out of it, and Bergé wants to avoid scandal most of all. The stolen painting will suddenly reappear, the whole thing can be explained away somehow by the cops, and Yves Saint Laurent can become the Patron Saint of French Charity."

"And what about the mysterious person who stole the painting in the first place?" Jean-Pierre said.

Séverine's cell phone rang. She looked at it, gasped and held it up: the call was from me!

I grabbed the phone. "Manon! Are you all right?" But the voice on the other end was male, a gruff, deep, menacing voice.

"There is no Manon!" the voice growled.

"Who is this? What do you mean?"

"There is only me and Pierrot."

"Who is this?!"

"Don't you recognize your old friend Harlequin?"

I looked at my friends in the Happy Elephant, whose eyes widened at my own horrified reaction. I put the cell phone on speaker so everyone could hear.

"Did you say your name was Harlequin?" I said.

"Pierrot cannot win," the voice said. "Columbina will be mine."

"Who's Columbina?"

"If you do not deliver the painting to me, you will never see your Manon alive again."

I didn't understand. If this mysterious caller had taken Manon hostage, then he surely also had the painting. Or where was it?

"Let me speak to Manon!"

"At the moment," the caller said, "she cannot talk to you."

"Please don't hurt her. What do you want us to do?"

"Bring the painting to the Grand Palais. Tonight, at midnight. You will find Manon waiting for you there."

"The Grand Palais? Are you joking?" The line beeped and then went silent. "Hello?" The mysterious Harlequin had hung up. "Note to self," I said. "Never ask a kidnapper who's pretending to be a medieval jester if he's joking."

Séverine picked up the phone and punched the "return call" button. She put the call on speaker phone, and we all listened while it rang.

"It must be a bluff," I said. "Either this guy has both Manon and the painting or neither. How could he end up with Manon and not the painting?"

"But he has your cell phone," Benoît said.

"You think this is the person who stole it in the first place?"

"Maybe, but why would he set up a ransom drop at the

Grand Palais?"

"Maybe it's the cops," said Jean-Pierre.

"No, the cops aren't going to set up a phony ransom drop. It's not how they work."

"The RMN?"

"Maybe," Benoît said, "but the RMN wouldn't tell us to make a hostage swap at the Grand Palais, even if they were doing a sting. No one would assume we were that stupid, and it would look bad for them if something went wrong."

The call finally went to voicemail, and we heard my own voice telling us to leave a message. Now Séverine's phone rang again: Manon's cell phone!

"Hello!" Séverine said. "Manon?"

For an endless moment, no one spoke. Finally, we heard a deep breath, and Harlequin spoke again. "Go to the sewer below the Grand Palais. Bring the painting. *De minuit, ce soir.* If you ever want to see Manon again!" The line beeped, and the man was gone.

"Midnight again," I said. "Why does everyone want to ransom their hostages at midnight?"

* * * * *

We sat for a while in the Happy Elephant, puzzling out what these new developments could possibly mean. Had Manon truly been taken hostage? The mysterious Harlequin had both of the mobile phones Manon had been carrying, but if she had been taken hostage, what had happened to *The Despair of Pierrot*?

At just after two o'clock in the afternoon, Séverine's cell phone rang again. It was Pierre Bergé. I answered it.

"I am calling as instructed, Monsieur Johnson. I agree to the terms of the exchange."

"What exchange?"

"Your agent called and asked me to meet you at a certain time at a certain place," he said discreetly. "I agree to it, but I certainly won't come myself. It's a lot of damn foolishness, to be frank, when you could simply come to my home, but I will send a representative to collect the item."

"My agent called you?" I said. "And who was my agent?"

Bergé exploded. "Enough games, Monsieur Johnson! I have agreed to everything. Now tell me where I should wire the money, and we can be rid of one another, once and for all!"

"One moment," I said. I muted the phone and quickly told the rest of the group what Bergé had said.

"It must be the cops," Jean-Pierre said. "They call us, they call him, they probably have Manon in custody. They're going to get everyone in the same place and arrest everyone."

"Johnson!" Bergé yelled through the phone.

Giselle motioned for me to give her the phone. I handed it to her, and she told Bergé the routing numbers to her Swiss bank account. She clicked off and reported that Bergé would transfer the money immediately and that he expected us to hand over "the item" at the appointed time and place or there would be consequences.

"Great," I said. "I love consequences."

Within the hour, Saanen Bank in Bern confirmed that Giselle had received a deposit of two and a half million euros. Now, all we had to do was find the painting, descend into the sewers directly below the Grand Palais in the middle of the night, survive *another* bogus hostage swap involving both Pierre Bergé and someone pretending to be a Commedia dell'Arte character, and rescue Manon, all without getting killed or leading the cops directly to the evidence that would put us all in prison.

This was not how I had imagined it would feel to be rich.

13

PIERROT REAPPEARS

Another hour of hand-wringing and brainstorming brought no new ideas. Benoît volunteered to go to the *Musée des Egouts* in the seventh arrondissement (the Sewer Museum—leave it to the Parisians to turn their own sewage system into a tourist attraction!) to get a map of the sewer network. He said he knew the sewers well personally, but he thought it important for the whole group to plot exact coordinates together—where to descend without coming too close to the Grand Palais above ground, good manholes where we could post sentries, potential escape routes and so on. He seemed delighted.

After her experience at Les Frigos, Séverine could not really believe that any of us would actually go into the sewers to meet two different groups of gun-toting crazies in a hostage exchange that was so obviously a set-up, and I tended to agree with her; but who exactly was being set up, and for what? Why had the mysterious Harlequin involved Bergé in this swap at all, and how had he known that he should pretend to act on my behalf when he called Bergé? Furthermore, this would be our second ransom exchange in which we had nothing at all to trade for the hostage, and one can only trust dumb luck so far.

The more time passed, the more we worried about Manon, and it became clearer and clearer that, all intrigue and curiosity aside, with no word from her and no painting in hand, we would eventually have to turn to the police, for sanity's sake. We were in over our heads, and if Manon's life were truly at stake, we would have to risk prison to save her. The cops would no doubt charge me, Giselle and Manon, at the very least, with obstructing their investigation. But that would be better than having Manon murdered at the hands of a psychotic Harlequin.

Once Benoît had departed for the Sewer Museum, Giselle and I decided to go home and get a little rest, and Séverine retired to her own apartment. We agreed to meet back at the Happy Elephant at around eight, hopefully with new ideas. As we walked up rue des Tournelles to my apartment, I spotted two men who seemed like plain-clothes policemen, at a *fromagerie*, smelling a wheel of yellow cheese.

* * * * *

Giselle flung herself down on my bed, and I slipped off my shoes and lay down beside her. We kissed and held one another for a while, and she told me how frightened she was that something dreadful had happened to Manon.

We mused for a while on Benoît's secret former life and how well he had managed to hide it from everyone, even in his most drunken ranting at the Happy Elephant. He had always seemed simply like a garbageman with a philosophical bent, nothing more, nothing less—which would not be the strangest thing in the world, not in Paris, where it's possible to find people of philosophical or artistic inclinations in nearly every profession. But to think of him as Napoleon le Tigre, having gay orgies with models and rock stars!

Eventually, I nodded off to sleep in Giselle's arms. I dreamed of Séverine naked and popped immediately awake again. Giselle petted my hair. As if she had been watching my dream, she said, "How did you patch things up with Séverine?"

"I didn't. Not exactly. She and Bergé know each other from

the times Séverine worked with Yves Saint Laurent, and Bergé asked to meet me at her shop, so I went. That's how we got back in touch."

"She seemed awfully friendly just now at the Elephant. It was as if nothing had happened at all, like old times. You must have talked to her about it."

"Well, she's with Eugene now," I evaded. "How long can you hold a grudge? Besides, these circumstances are rather extraordinary, so maybe she thought it was a good time to let bygones be bygones. To live in the present."

"She was looking at you in a way that made me extremely jealous," Giselle said.

"Well." I turned to look her square in the face. "It's complicated."

She drew in a sharp breath. "You didn't sleep with her, Luke? Tell me you didn't!"

"No, I didn't."

I thought of the salad greens Séverine had woven into her hair the night we went to Les Frigos; of her sitting naked on her sofa next to me, drinking armagnac; of holding her close as we lay in her bed last night, her back expanding and contracting against my chest with each gentle breath. Was all that nothing? Was kissing her nothing? And yet, what did it amount to, next to Giselle here in my bed, in my arms, as we lay together in a disquietingly similar position? Hadn't that just been nostalgia and pain and relief and exhaustion with Séverine, a way to reach closure? How would I feel, I asked myself, if Giselle had done those same things with an ex-lover?

"No, I didn't sleep with her. She told me that she was happy with Eugene, and I told her I was happy with you, and we congratulated each other on our relationships. It's good that this all happened, I think, that we can finally put the past behind us. She was a trooper at Les Frigos."

Giselle continued to search my eyes, challenging me to tell her the whole truth. A knock came at the door.

"Monsieur Johnson!" It was the building concierge. I got out of bed, checked the peephole to make sure she was alone and opened the door. Over a matronly gray dress, she wore a white apron mottled with stains from ancient sauces, and she had an almost comically worried look on her face. "Monsieur Johnson," she said guiltily. "I am doing a terrible thing."

"What is it?"

"The police told me to keep an eye on you, to call them if anything suspicious happened. Of course, I told them I would. But..." She shrugged. "I've known you for twelve years, Monsieur. I know you are honest." I blushed when she said this and glanced over my shoulder at Giselle, who had gotten out of bed. "Tell me truthfully. Are you involved in something that you shouldn't be?"

"Yes, Madame Corbin. But I've done nothing illegal. Not at all. I am involved completely against my will. It has to do with—"

She held up her hand. "Don't tell me. I know how these things happen." She leaned in closer and lowered her voice. "You see, my father fought in the Battle of Algiers."

The Battle of Algiers was the name for a long series of guerilla skirmishes between French troops and Algerian nationalists in the Algerian war for independence in the 1950s. I could only guess that her father had become involved in something immoral or illegal against his will, which had been common enough in that war.

"I like having you live here in my building, Monsieur Johnson. You are a gentleman."

I thanked her. "But what is it, Madame Corbin? Why are you asking me this? What have you done?"

"A package has arrived for you." My heart leapt. "I told the police I would report to them, but… I don't want to, Monsieur. As long as you give me your word that what they say isn't true."

"What do they say?"

"They say you stole that painting from the Grand Palais."

"No, Madame Corbin, it isn't true." I put my hand over my racing heart.

"Will you open the package in front of me, to show me that I'm right to place my trust in you? That I have nothing to worry about?"

I looked at Giselle. Her eyes were wide with excitement and curiosity. I said, "Of course."

Madame Corbin turned and descended the stairs, and we followed her to her office on the ground floor. There, sitting on her desk, was a large wicker-weave picnic basket with a red ribbon tied around its handle! A card knotted onto the ribbon said, "Dalloyau," the name of a chain of upscale catering and specialty food shops scattered around Paris. Dalloyau had been in business since the reign of Louis XIV, and they made fancy macaroons and sumptuous quiches and every kind of rich chocolate and baked delicacy: it was upper-class fingerfood, too expensive for everyday Parisians, the kind of food royals eat when they're just noshing. I untied the ribbon and opened the basket, and we all peered inside.

It contained probably five hundred euros' worth of treats: a pencil box filled with tiny jars of tapanade, rosemary-mint water crackers, a variety of macaroons in a patterned baking sleeve, single-serving quiches, cups of salmon mousse, a black plastic tray holding two veal cutlets under a clear plastic cover, duck foie gras, a pair of *quatr'heure* caramel pastries and, to top off this feast, a bottle of Veuve Clicquot. Everything nestled into a folded red and white checkered picnic blanket at the bottom of the basket, a blanket that seemed gigantic, as if, spread out on a lawn, it would accommodate not just a pair of picnickers but their horse, as well. I mashed my palm down hard into the blanket, pretending for Madame Corbin's benefit to be searching for more hidden delicacies. Something was folded into it!

"Looks like dinner," I said cheerily.

"Oh, Monsieur, how silly!" Madame Corbin's face relaxed into a smile and then a laugh.

"But what did you think it could be?" I asked, teasing. "It's from Dalloyau!"

"I don't know," Madame Corbin laughed again. "A bomb maybe!"

"Read the card," said Giselle.

A scribble that was shaky but unmistakably Manon's said, "Please accept my apologies for these unfortunate misunderstandings. Cordially, Pierre Bergé." I read the note aloud and the concierge laughed again and put her hand over her heart.

"Here, Madame Corbin." I motioned for her to select from among the delicacies. "I see by your apron that you're making dinner, but maybe you'd like a little appetizer?"

"No, no, Monsieur, it isn't necessary."

"Nonsense! We can't eat all this food ourselves." I selected a salmon mousse, an onion quiche and a sleeve of macaroons for Madame Corbin, who laughed and blushed and continued to say no, no, she couldn't. When I had emptied half of the contents of the basket onto her desk, I said, solemnly, "Thank you for believing in me, Madame." I shook her hand.

"I knew it must be a misunderstanding!"

I closed the basket, thanked Madame Corbin again and walked as casually as possible back up to my apartment with Giselle. When we had locked the door behind us, I unloaded the fancy food in a heap onto my desk and shook the checkered blanket out on my bed. It unfolded with some difficulty, the two of us pulling and shaking it. I could feel something cool and thick beneath the acrylic fleece. Finally, we wrestled it all the way open and, with an audible little flop, it disgorged a canvas onto the bed. *The Despair of Pierrot*!

* * * * *

The canvas was ragged around the edges where it had been cut from its frame, but otherwise it was in perfect condition, exactly as it had looked in the slideshow I had seen in Joseph Danton's office. The scene was breathtaking in its misery, with heavy strokes of orange, black and red for Pierrot's hair, which echoed the blackened orange circles under his eyes: his whole head was a dark fire of desolation. The cobalt blue sky behind him created a peaceful backdrop, against which the horrifyingly blank expressions of the colorful masks on the Commedia dell'Arte characters around Pierrot seemed all the more mocking. It was a devastating statement of the insufficiency of humor to cope with anguish. It made beauty out of the unending grief of Pierrot in the face of the heartless frivolity of his companions.

"It's marvelously grim," Giselle whispered.

We had the painting, thanks to Manon, but she had sacrificed herself in the bargain. We now had to smuggle the canvas past the gauntlet of police waiting for us outside and manage a hostage exchange. "I still can't help feeling that something is wrong here."

"Lots of things are wrong here, Luke!"

"No, I mean, we have Bergé's money, so we could give him the painting and that would make sense. Or we could give Harlequin the painting in exchange for Manon, and that would make sense. But if Harlequin and Bergé both show up tonight, someone is going to leave empty-handed. Why would

Harlequin pretend to be us in order to invite Bergé to this rendezvous? It's the same as the meeting at Les Frigos: someone is being set up."

"Do you think Harlequin has another motive, then? What if he wants to kill Bergé?"

"But Bergé won't even be there. Jacques Martin is in prison, so it can't be him." I pushed the canvas aside and sat down on the bed. "Harlequin figures out that Manon has the painting and chases her, but she manages to duck into Dalloyau and hide the painting and have it delivered to us. Then Harlequin picks up her scent again and she jumps down a manhole to try to escape, like Jean Valjean, but Harlequin nabs her anyway. Then, seizing on this idea of the sewers, he arranges a rendezvous directly beneath the scene of the crime, and invites the victim of his original theft, Pierre Bergé, to the ransom swap? No, it doesn't even begin to add up."

Giselle and I stared at the painting, but it kept its secrets. "Too bad we can't just keep it," she said. "It really is spectacular."

"I'd just as soon have the two and a half million, if it's all the same to you." I looked at the heap of delicacies on my desk. "Well, we should fortify ourselves for tonight. Cheers to Manon for the feast, anyway." Leave it to Manon, in the heat of a day-long chase across Paris, on the run from the police and a dangerous criminal, to camouflage a stolen painting inside a beautiful selection of gourmet treats.

"She does have flair, doesn't she? We'll save the champagne to share with her."

"Sure," I said, as optimistically as I could. "She'll be wanting a midnight snack when this is over."

I called Jean-Pierre and told him to get a message to everyone else, to meet at my apartment instead of the Happy Elephant. I didn't risk telling him why over the phone, and he didn't ask. We took the painting into the bathroom and draped it over the shower curtain rod, and then we spread the checkered blanket on my bed and laid out our picnic. Giselle took one bite of the veal cutlet and broke into tears.

"Oh, Luke!"

I took her in my arms. "It'll be okay."

"Will it?"

"She'll be okay. We won't let anything happen to her."

"They just want the painting, right?"

"We'll give them the painting. They won't hurt her. They won't need to."

14

COMMEDIA DELL'ARTE

At just after eight, Benoît and Séverine arrived separately at my apartment. Séverine had changed yet again: she vamped in wearing a gray military overcoat with silver and black epaulets, topped off with a faux general's hat complete with military stars and ribbons. She hung the coat and hat on hooks near my front door, revealing, underneath, a gray corset-style top cinched tight in the back with black laces, and a matching mini-skirt with extravagantly fake military ribbons at the hips. Her black tights were spangled with tiny silver French Army stars. The only part of her outfit that didn't seem like dominatrix gear were her boots, which were actual black leather work boots, practical rather than sexy, though somehow even these seemed risqué. Giselle looked mildly scandalized and turned an incredulous look toward me behind Séverine's back. Benoît, uncontroversially, wore his green City of Paris coveralls.

"Have you seen a television this evening?" Séverine said. "Everyone's yammering about the auction. They've run the security camera video from the Grand Palais about a thousand times—the one of the painting vanishing into thin air—and France 2 has a security expert analyzing a diagram of the Grand Palais' electrical wiring. I just saw Joseph Danton answering questions on France Direct, and Canal Plus is showing a documentary about Yves Saint Laurent."

I took them into the bathroom and showed them *The Despair of Pierrot* hanging over my shower rod. "Let's try not to appear on television ourselves, eh?"

After Séverine and Benoît had finished admiring the painting, we got down to the business of planning how to get rid of it. Benoît produced a map of the sewers and spread it on my bed. I took one look at its quaint fonts and fake-parchment borders and knew something was wrong—the legend read 1878!

"It's a souvenir from a museum, Luke, not a plan from the Public Works Department. You can't just buy a current plan of the entire sewer system. Anyway, the Grand Palais is right downtown—the tunnels won't have changed in that area."

We studied the nineteenth century diagram of the vast intestines of Paris. Since it seemed obvious to me that none of us could leave my apartment with the painting and then openly descend with it into the sewers, I began tracing an underground route from my apartment to the Grand Palais. "Do you think we could make it all the way from the basement of this building through the sewers?" I asked.

"No," said Benoît. "There's probably no access from this building. Service entrances are usually manholes in the streets." He pointed on the map at a manhole at the Place des Vosges, around the corner. "Or sometimes there are trap doors in the basements of large businesses or public buildings." He studied the map some more and located a symbol for a service access beneath the Castidines Hotel on the Canal Saint Martin, nearly a kilometer away in the wrong direction. He put his nose down near the map and hovered over it, squinting.

"Any chance there could be an access through the Happy Elephant?"

"The wine cellar!" Giselle said.

"Maybe," said Benoît doubtfully. "Call Jean-Pierre."

Séverine called on her mobile phone. Jean-Pierre reported that there was, indeed, a set of wooden trap doors in the floor of his wine cellar, but that they only connected to the basement boiler room of his building.

"Tell him to go into the boiler room and look around," Benoît said. "According to this map, there isn't another man-hole on this street, so there could be an access down there." He helped himself to the last onion quiche. "I wonder what kind of business was there before Jean-Pierre moved in."

"It was a silversmith," Giselle said. "*Bijoutier Lambert.* Jewelry, silverware, antiques. It used to take up the whole first floor of his building."

"Lambert?" said Benoît. "Jewish probably. Makes sense in the Marais. Might have been there since the Revolution. Sounds promising."

While we waited for Jean-Pierre to call back with his findings, I suggested one possibility for this evening that we had not yet explored, an idea I thought we might at least try before we gave ourselves over completely to Harlequin's demands: an alliance with Pierre Bergé. "He's not going to get the painting back under these circumstances, anyway," I pointed out. "We're going to give it to Harlequin! But if Bergé throws his lot in with us, we could gang up on Harlequin, and we could all come out of this clean. Catch Harlequin at his own game and turn him over to the cops. The police 'solve' the crime and get the real criminal, Bergé gets his painting back, we rescue Manon and keep the money: everyone's happy!"

"That's not a bad thought," Séverine said.

Séverine called Bergé and explained what was happening, to the best of our understanding, and offered him an alliance. After listening for a while, Bergé exploded in a volley of fury so loud and obscene that we all heard his fomentations clearly through Séverine's earpiece.

"It seems he doesn't trust us," said Séverine, when Bergé finally hung up. "When I said that Manon's kidnapper called himself Harlequin, Bergé asked if I would put Scaramouche on the phone, so that he could negotiate with the gang directly."

"At least he has an admirable grasp of Commedia dell'Arte characters."

* * * * *

Benoît pointed out all the manholes on the map near the Grand Palais. "But it would obviously be better," he said, "to take the painting straight into the sewers from the Happy Elephant. It would be a long walk underground, but that way I could go directly to the rendezvous spot unseen, and the cops would believe I had remained in the bar drinking. Jean-Pierre could even provide an alibi."

Benoît retrieved the canvas from my bathroom, rolled it up and slipped it awkwardly into his coveralls, where it made obscene bulges. With an overcoat and some nonchalant walking, he could appear perfectly normal to anyone observing him on the streets.

Jean-Pierre telephoned and reported that he had found a set of double steel doors in the floor of his building's basement. They were heavily chained and padlocked and seemed, judging by the rust all over them, not to have been opened in a hundred years.

"Maybe our luck is changing," I said.

Benoît waggled his eyebrows. "Got a bolt cutter and some oil?"

I sneaked down into my own building's basement and snooped among the tools that Madame Corbin and her husband kept there. I couldn't find bolt cutters, but I did take a battery powered Dremel—a handheld rotary saw—and a pair of heavy pliers. I climbed the stairs silently back to my apartment, where everyone was finishing off Manon's picnic and chatting about the television news coverage they had seen of the heist.

I changed into some waterproof boots and found a headlamp that I sometimes took with me into war zones. I tried the light, and it glowed bright and blue. I put it, my Swiss Army knife, my borrowed tools and the SIG Sauer I had removed from Bergé's lieutenant into my overcoat pockets. I pulled a black skullcap down over my ears and slipped on a pair of winter gloves, and then walked back and forth a few steps, testing the swing and sway of my coat with the tools and weapons as ballast.

The possibility that Harlequin simply wanted to lure all of us down into the sewers to murder us and escape with the painting darkened my thoughts, but it was too late to be afraid now. Everyone bundled up in warm clothing, and we walked slowly down rue des Tournelles toward the Happy Elephant.

The snowstorm that had been threatening all day had finally let loose, with so many chunky flakes that the buildings on my block seemed like giant *mille-feuilles* dusted with powdered sugar. I stuck out my tongue and caught a fat flake, and Benoît scowled at me.

"We are not on a school field trip," he said.

One thing you learn when photographing firefights is how to keep yourself fresh and alert for the moment of action, mainly by allowing yourself some lighthearted enjoyment during the times in-between. I caught another snowflake and stuck my tongue out at Benoît, so he could see it melt. Benoît rolled his eyes.

The street was empty now, yellow lights shining through the windows of nearly every apartment, our fellow Parisians huddling into the doughy warmth inside while our shoes crunched the snow crusting the sidewalk. A single car rolled past, blacking the pristine street with grime, but the passengers were a harmless looking older couple staring fixedly at the transformed road. We talked loudly about everyday things for the benefit of anyone observing or listening; and we formed a little triangle around Benoît, to conceal any gracelessness in his gait caused by the hidden canvas. We arrived at the Happy Elephant at just after nine-thirty.

Fortunately, no other drinkers had braved the storm tonight. Benoît went into the bathroom and removed the canvas from his coveralls, while Jean-Pierre laid out some miscellaneous supplies on the bar, which he had scrounged from his storeroom: a headlamp, a length of rope, and two mismatched nylon shoe covers. "To protect your feet from the sewers," he said, making a disgusted face.

"No need for the sour face," Benoît said, emerging again from the bathroom. "The sewers are mainly storm drains, now. Since the nineteenth century, most human waste goes into pipes suspended from the tops of the tunnels. It'll just be snow melt and dog shit tonight."

Jean-Pierre made another disgusted face. "Always the silver lining, eh, Benoît?"

"We step in dog shit every day," said Benoît. "This is Paris!"

Benoît descended into the basement boiler room with my landlady's Dremel, to see if the doors Jean-Pierre had found truly led to the sewers. Jean-Pierre poured us all a round of drinks, and we sipped them, mainly for show; and then he turned up the volume on the sound system, to mask our voices in the event that the RMN was eavesdropping electronically. After ten minutes or so, Benoît climbed out of the wine cellar, sweating generously, and announced that we had access to the sewers!

"They're flowing quite strong tonight, with all of this snow," he said. He turned to Jean-Pierre. "Do you have any plastic wrap, to protect the painting?" Jean-Pierre found a roll of plastic wrap, and Benoît went into the bathroom to roll a length of it around the canvas.

Jean-Pierre stroked his beard and said, "I'm going to give Benoît my mobile phone, Luke. You should take Giselle's or Séverine's—you'll need to keep in touch, in case there's trouble."

"You think there'll be a signal in the sewers?"

"You can always get a signal in the metro, so why not?"

"Okay, I'll take Séverine's. She already has Bergé's number in her contact list, and Harlequin knows to call her in order to reach us, so I can be in touch with everyone that way." Séverine handed me her cell phone, and I programmed Jean-Pierre's mobile and the Happy Elephant's landline as speed dial numbers.

No matter how well or poorly we prepared ourselves now, I thought, we would essentially be at the mercy of forces beyond our control once we entered the sewers. As if reading my mind, Giselle said, "Try not to do anything risky tonight, all right? And don't shoot anyone! Just do what they say and get Manon out of there."

At ten o'clock, Séverine wished us all *bon courage* and headed out into the snowstorm toward the train for Maison-Alfort. Her only job this evening was to stay far away from trouble and, with luck, to take some surveillance with her to the opposite side of town. Giselle cast a last dubious glance at Séverine's military fetish uniform, as Séverine flounced around the corner, catwalk-high-stepping in her work boots on the icy sidewalk. She looked like an amateur showgirl.

"Are you sure you don't want to tell me anything about that?" Giselle said.

"I'm not sure what to say about it myself."

Five minutes later, it was Giselle's turn to be off. She kissed me and held me tight for a long moment before buttoning up her coat and setting her teeth against the cold. She headed toward the St. Paul metro station, to venture off in the opposite direction from Séverine toward Aubervilliers.

"Jean-Pierre," I said. "I'm getting déjà vu." Hadn't we all just met at the Happy Elephant the day before for a hostage rescue mission? Hadn't we all taken different routes in order to shake any police surveillance or other pursuers? "We shouldn't do this!"

"What do you mean?" Jean-Pierre said.

"That thing Manon said, about a clue being hidden in the painting itself. I think she was right! I just didn't realize *how* she was right until right now!"

"What do you mean?"

"We're doing everything all over again, just like before! Don't you see? Harlequin? He even invoked Columbina on the phone. Pierrot?"

"You mean we're playing out a Commedia dell'Arte plot?" Jean-Pierre said.

"Exactly! It's Commedia dell'Arte. We've done all of this already! The hostages. The swap for the painting. The mysterious third party. The same plot plays out over and over again with variations, but it always has the same characters and it always ends the same! We're acting out *The Despair of Pierrot!*"

"It's not a bad theory, but how would that really be possible? Who would be staging the drama and why? It seems to me that Harlequin said he was Harlequin just to be nasty. To mock us."

I wasn't sure how to carry my idea any further, or what it might mean, even, if we really were trapped in some medieval farce. I punched the internet browser on Séverine's phone and waited a short eternity until a search window opened and then typed in Commedia dell'Arte, but nothing useful came up that we didn't already know.

Jean-Pierre said, "The fact that something similar happens twice doesn't necessarily mean it's a pattern. It could be a coincidence."

"I'm ready," Benoît called from the bathroom. He opened the door and came out on his hands and knees. He moved in herky-jerky fits, trying to protect the canvas hidden under his clothes.

"Commedia dell'Arte is a set of conventions too specific to reproduce in the real world," Jean-Pierre continued. "It's not possible. Too many variables."

Benoît said, "What would you call the repetition of historical events, then? For example, the Paris Commune of 1871 and the Paris Uprising of 1968, two nearly identical failed revolutions a hundred years apart that arose out of nearly identical circumstances?"

"But they didn't rely on stock types in conventional structures with clearly defined narrative aims. The similarities weren't metaphorical! They were the result of the students' unwillingness to learn from history, and so they just made similar mistakes. It's not the same at all!"

Benoît shrugged. He got down on the floor and crawled between tables and chairs, shielding himself as much as possible from the plate glass windows on rue des Tournelles. He wriggled behind the bar and slid Jean-Pierre's headlamp onto his head. "We'll find out how metaphorical it all is beneath the Grand Palais at midnight." He climbed down the wooden ladder out of sight. "Call me in fifteen minutes, and we'll see if we can get a signal down in the sewer." He closed the cellar door and was gone.

Jean-Pierre and I stared out at the snow, falling thicker and heavier now than ever, hitting the Happy Elephant's windows and sliding in great, half-frozen rivulets toward the sidewalk. "If no one calls me by 12:30am," he said, "I'm calling the police."

"That's exactly what you said before!" My skin crawled.

"Well, the rendezvous is at midnight, just like before."

I nearly flapped my arms in frustration. It was déjà vu all over again; but this time, I thought, the ending to the drama would change. I clutched the SIG Sauer in my overcoat pocket and strode purposefully out of the Happy Elephant.

15

The Sewer

I followed Giselle's footsteps in the snow down rue des Tournelles to rue de Rivoli, where they joined a more general slush of indifference mucking up the sidewalk. A few taxis were parked with their motors running and their tailpipes steaming, and cars and trucks rumbled sporadically along increasingly well-defined tracks through the accumulating snow. This street was usually bristling with chatter and flying elbows day and night, but now it was hushed and lonely. A pair of wizened old Orthodox Jewish men, with long gray beards, flat black hats and black overcoats, stood out against the shavings of white sky swirling around them. They inclined their heads toward one another, deep in contemplation and heedless of the inclimate weather, and I imagined that they were not elders of their community but well-disguised policemen tracking my movements out of the corners of their eyes. Everyone seemed like a character in a play.

I ran across the street in front of St. Paul Cathedral toward the metro stop. The snow turned the steps leading down into the subway into a Slip'n Slide, the nighttime travelers clinging to the handrails as they descended. I opened the door to the metro tunnel, and warm, urine-smelling air blasted out.

I dialed Benoît. "*Oui*," he answered immediately. His voice echoed, thin and distant.

"*Alors*?"

"*Bien*." He clicked off.

I hurried down the tunnel and jumped into a train heading

west. It was a quarter till eleven. So far so good.

* * * * *

When I emerged from the Concorde stop, I saw the giant Obelisk of Luxor in the center of the *place*. Its red granite seemed black against the snow. I walked toward rue Royale, scanning the open plaza: a few people went shuffling toward the Champs-Élysées, but, for the moment, the pedestrian commons around the obelisk was a blank, snow-white page still waiting for a story. No one seemed to mark me as I turned north toward the Madeleine Church, whose white-columned arrogance seemed heightened by the blinding white night. Based on the Pantheon in Athens, the church was originally designed as a faux Greek glorification of Napoleon's conquests, and it still seemed more a call to arms than to worship. The dome near the back of the church seemed like Napoleon's own bald pate defying god. Somewhere near the church's northwestern corner, my portal into the underworld awaited.

Benoît had told me that all of the sewer portals in the city that weren't located directly in the middle of streets were marked by steel balls, like larger versions of the knobs you find on fireplace andirons. I scanned the street where rue Chavreau Lagarde intersected rue Tronchet. A shiny yellow Smart coupé motored down the avenue, took the turn a little too fast and fishtailed away. I searched the church's foundations for perfectly rounded little snow heaps or balls protruding from the otherwise uniform blanket of white. In a little stretch of open space between the cobblestones of the Place Madeleine and the sidewalk, nearly hidden between two snow-draped shrubs, I spotted three small mounds in a suspiciously symmetrical triangle.

I ducked down behind the shrubs and slapped at a

rounded heap with my gloved hand. The snow scattered, revealing a steel ball: just as Benoît had described! The other two snowballs also revealed steel underneath, all three connected to a heavy black manhole cover. The balls acted as both markers and handles. I grabbed one with both hands and lifted. It resisted momentarily, but with a little effort, the cover scooted up and off. The smell of ammonia belched out into the cold night. I felt elated at this quick success. Of course, I still had half a kilometer to cover through the sewers.

I checked the time on Séverine's mobile phone: ten minutes past eleven. It seemed a little too early to descend. I decided to take cover for a few minutes in the shadows at the rear of the Madeleine, near the corner of the church. I dialed Benoît.

"*Pas mal*," he reported. "The water is freezing, and the rats are confused by the storm, so they're more aggressive than usual, but otherwise it's all right. I had to detour around some construction, so I'll come at the spot from the north now, but nothing to worry about. Don't call me from now on unless there's an emergency."

I crouched in the blackness below the Madeleine. The snowstorm might have been our best piece of luck: with almost no one on the street, it would be easy to identify anyone who might approach my hiding place. From my vantage point against the building, I was invisible to passersby, yet I could clearly see the whole plaza and the manhole cover.

The few people crossing the plaza on foot all seemed to be in a hurry. This was an area of luxury hotels and coldly grand monuments, not the sort of space that encouraged wintertime frolics. One person approached alone, then two separate pairs, coming from the direction of Boulevard Malesherbes and crossing toward Place Vendôme. I was suspicious of everyone, but no one even glanced at the Madeleine.

I was thinking it was time to creep toward the manhole,

when a figure in uniform loomed suddenly out of the snow to my right, walking directly toward the church. I crouched down into myself, trying to become smaller in the shadows. It seemed to be a policeman, judging by the hat and coat, but then, a distinctive sway of hips made it seem more like a policewoman instead. The figure came closer and closer, approaching with caution, marked more and more clearly as a woman by her gait. The closer she came, the more hesitantly she walked, but she was looking for something near where I was squatting. I saw a riot club swing out from her right hand. I held my breath. She still did not see me, though she was just a couple of meters away.

It's over, I thought. I would give up on venturing down into the sewers and just walk away across the *place*: no sense leading the cops right to *The Despair of Pierrot*. I stood up cautiously, and the woman hissed, "Luke, is that you?"

My heart sank. "Séverine?" Her military dominatrix gear, especially the epauletted overcoat, looked convincingly official in the dark. "What the hell are you doing here?"

"Luke, thank God I found you." She hurried forward and joined me in the shadows. "I came to settle something. About you and me, Luke. Once and for all."

"We're in the middle of a hostage rescue operation!"

"I saw what happened last time, at Les Frigos," she said. "You could easily be killed tonight, and I won't let you die without resolving this."

I stared past her across the open *place*. "You know, the whole point of your going to Maison-Alforts was to take the cops *away* from the rendezvous site! Did you at least notice if anyone followed you?"

"Actually, someone did, but I lost him at Montparnasse." She held out her closed fist. Reluctantly, I opened my hand. She deposited an iPod with a set of earphones in my gloved palm. "I made you something. It's a recording. Of me. Listen to it."

"Now?"

"You have some distance to walk before you get to the Grand Palais, right? The recording isn't long. I made it for you this evening."

"You want me to listen to a recording you made about our relationship while I walk through the sewers?"

"Why not? Just take it. If everything turns out all right tonight and you want to talk about it later, we'll talk. If not, well…" She looked down at her feet. "I'll be satisfied."

Watching a woman in dominatrix gear cry has an oddly alienating effect. "I have to go now," I said.

She wrapped her arms around my neck, pressed the whole length of her body against me and whispered, "Be careful," the words warm and wet in my ear. She kissed my neck and then stepped back. Tears rolled down her cheeks.

"As long as you're here, why don't you walk across the street and keep watch while I go into the sewer?" She nodded. "Yell if you see anyone coming. If I can't get the manhole cover back on from inside, come back over in a few minutes and replace it."

"Promise me you'll listen?"

"I'll try."

I put the iPod in my pocket, but Séverine reached in for it, fished out the tiny earbuds and stuck them into my ears. She then whirled and walked briskly out to the middle of the street. She crossed toward the dormant fountain in the plaza west of the church, and when she was in place, she nonchalantly lifted and lowered her arm, as if she were adjusting her clothing. I waited until a black Mercedes sped past toward rue Royale and then walked to the manhole cover. I looked up toward Séverine: she raised and lowered her arm again and adjusted her hat. We should have established what these signals meant ahead of time, I thought.

The fetid stench of the sewer rose to greet me. Down in the hole, pitch blackness waited. I lowered myself in and my foot found the first rung of a metal ladder set into sandstone walls. When I had climbed just below street level, I reached back up for the cover but couldn't budge it: my feet felt uncertain on the wet, slippery rungs; my angle toward the cover was awkward. I abandoned it to Séverine. Perhaps her ill-advised attempt to have a last tête-à-tête about our relationship would actually be the thing that kept the police from discovering us in the sewers.

I pulled my headlamp onto my forehead and turned it on. The light revealed slimy, wet, mottled gray walls. The cold damp of the rusted rungs went straight through my gloves, straight through my skin to my bones. I extended one leg down and my foot found the next rung, then the next, and I passed one hand over another until I had descended seven or eight meters. The farther I went, the more claustrophobic the tunnel became, and the sound of rushing water below became louder and stronger. The smell of skunk spray over rotting eggs and the stinking corruption of decomposing flesh pushed into my nose like solid objects. The sewers were like sausage tubes filled with the off-gassing of old diarrhea and sulfur. Jets of saliva streamed into my mouth, and I clinched my jaws compulsively. I was drooling.

I felt a shadow cross over me, and I looked up to see a figure appear in the hole overhead: Séverine. She waved and then the hole disappeared slowly, like an eclipse of the moon.

It was only when the meager light and fresh air from above had been completely blocked that the deep, terrifying strangeness of the sewer hit me. It wasn't just the odor that made it so horrible—it was the feeling of being in the very intestines of some great, awful beast. I tried not to think of all the effluvium that had passed through these tunnels since the 1300s.

I reached the bottom of the ladder and found myself in a stone tube perpendicular to the one I had climbed down and parallel to the street up above. It was a few feet taller than I was and wide enough so that I could have stretched out both of my arms fully and my fingertips would have just touched both sides; but I hesitated to step off of the last rung of the ladder, because of the dark flowing liquid completely covering the bottom. My light on the water reflected agitated darkness back at me.

I reached into my pocket to make sure the SIG Sauer was handy, and I accidentally hit the play button on Séverine's iPod. I nearly slipped off the last rung of the ladder as her voice came blasting into my head. I pressed my gloved finger randomly all over the little device till the volume decreased and then it stopped altogether.

I tested my footing against a stone at the edge of the water. It would be impossible to stand with both feet on the near side because the curve of the tunnel was too severe, and yet I thought the water a little too wide to straddle. I would have to step directly down into it. I braced myself for the cold, braced for the force of the surging liquid and stepped down.

The frigid water hit my ankle. My bones turned to ice.

I lowered my other foot and stood with my knees bent for a moment to make sure of my balance. I found that, in fact, the curve of the tunnel just allowed me to stand with one foot on either side of the rushing water. The half a kilometer to the Grand Palais now seemed like a million miles, but I set off walking, each wet step an awkward challenge. I directed my light up along the length of the tunnel. A host of metal pipes, plastic tubes and insulated cables twisted along the ceiling.

Almost immediately, I came to a cross tunnel, a kind of

smaller tributary splashing its runoff into my tunnel, and I saw that, above this crossroads, blue signs with white lettering announced the names of the streets overhead. Rue d'Anjou. A good start: I began to feel a little more sane.

My progress became quicker as I became more accustomed to the angle of the stones, and I decided that it might not be a bad idea to listen to Séverine's message now, after all. Better that than think about what nastiness was splashing by between my legs or the many potential catastrophes awaiting all of us at the rendezvous. I felt for the iPod and found the play button.

Séverine's cooing despair made my head swim. I wondered if I would forever after associate her voice with the sewers, surely not an effect she would want.

She talked briefly about how she had felt when she'd first seen me at her shop a few days before, with Pierre Bergé, and then she went into a stream-of-consciousness ramble that led her back to the first heady days of our relationship. It began innocuously enough, as any lover's memories might, telling a tale of early hope and eventual heartbreak, but then her story took a rather remarkable turn. She told me that, since our relationship had ended, she had found a new dimension to her sexuality and desires with Eugene, and she confessed a series of increasingly outré fetishes, starting with role-playing and moving through bondage, sado-masochism and humiliation rituals, which she described in detail. She could almost have been describing Benoît's experiences as Napoleon le Tigre in the underground sex culture of the 1970s. She said that now she longed more than ever to be with me, to explore these new desires—not with Eugene but with me!—and would that make coming back to her any more tantalizing? She thought it would deepen our intimacy and our connection if I humiliated her sexually in various ways, and she described a particular fantasy in incredibly graphic detail. Her voice, as she said these things, was filled with gleeful anomie, a sing-songy kind of gloom, and I suddenly realized by a little moan that seemed to escape her involuntarily, that Séverine had been masturbating while she made this recording! Now, she stopped talking altogether and instead was groaning and gasping. She recorded the entire experience, a relatively brief and breathless cascade of haunted whimpers. She had just had sex in my ears!

After a brief pause, she returned to the narrative of her life, and her voice became even more emotional. She told me how little meaning her life had had without me, describing the sense of loneliness that she still felt every day, even after two years, whenever she touched anything in her apartment that she knew I had touched before (in other words, almost every object she owned). It was as if, she said, the memory of me was the only thing that kept her feeling anything at all. Now that I was back in her life, even under these dreadful circumstances, the colors were more vibrant, the tastes more intense and her body more alive. The details of her sadness were embarrassing, and I wondered if she took pleasure in the thought of my feeling embarrassed for her. Was this just another humiliation ritual or was it all true, and it only just happened to be humiliating?

The recording ended, and I dropped the iPod into the sewer.

* * * * *

I soldiered on through the tunnel. The Grand Palais and the Madeleine were both practically on the Seine, and a major tunnel ran almost directly between them, mimicking the course of the river in a graceful curve. This tunnel would join another such major effluent transom from the 16th arrondissement near the Trocadero, where the by-then-raging torrent of runoff would be mechanically pumped to the western suburb of Clichy for treatment. Here, the waters still flowed according to gravity and the engineered slope of the tunnel, meaning that I was walking downhill the entire way, a stress that I began to feel in my knees.

I reached the turn I had to take. Unlike the labyrinthine switchbacks and detours that Benoît was navigating, I was required to make only one turn, at Avenue Edward Tuck, which, according to Benoît's map, would lead me right under the Grand Palais. This tunnel was quite a bit smaller than the one I had been negotiating. As I had listened to Séverine's dolorous sexual escapade, I had become accustomed, almost unconsciously, to walking with my feet at oddly curved angles, but I found that I could not straddle the water beneath Avenue Edward Tuck: the sides of the narrow tunnel were too acutely angled and the water too high. I would have to walk directly in the middle of the stream of muck. I stepped in with care. The frigid water lapped painfully at my calves.

A rat hit my right leg. It tried to clamber up my pants but I kicked violently, banging the toe of my boot into the side of the sewer, sending the rat flying. My left foot slid. The rat squealed and plopped back into the water, which carried it away, and I tottered backwards. I planted my foot and steadied myself with both hands against the sides of the tunnel. The pain of the kick reverberated through my freezing toes. Now, in addition to the odor of dog shit and vomit flowing through the tunnel, I smelled disaster: how were we ever going to accomplish anything under these conditions? How would Benoît protect the painting through kilometers of such hazards? More importantly, who would choose such a Styx of watery filth to exchange a priceless masterpiece of Expressionist art—wasn't this Harlequin figure worried about ruining the thing he desired most?

I forced myself to concentrate on each step, on the runny animal droppings, street grit and liquid trash of Paris's streets slithering around my ankles. It seemed the sound of the water was changing, becoming slightly higher pitched. I was closing in on the Grand Palais. I noticed a change in the movement of air, as well. I saw, up ahead, a large cross tunnel with a light shining through it. I switched off my headlamp. For the third time, I reached for the SIG Sauer in my pocket, and this time I pulled it out and took the safety off.

* * * * *

My feet had become nothing more than icy molds filling my leaden boots—hobo ice sculptures. I stood at the entrance to the cross tunnel. It was large and well lit with bluish light: curiously, the water from the tunnel where I now stood rushed strongly into the larger tunnel and flowed away to the left, toward the Seine; but the effluvium coming from the right, from the much larger tunnel in front of me, was nothing more than a trickle, despite the fact that the entire 16th arrondissement should have been emptying into it.

I stepped into the cross tunnel and walked a few paces toward the blinding blue light. I saw a figure up ahead, leaning against the side of the tunnel, and I raised my pistol. After a few more steps, I saw that it was a woman. My heartbeat quickened. She was wearing a mask that completely covered her face and an elaborately ruffled red dress with petticoats. She was dressed for a masked ball!

"Manon?" I said. My voice was swallowed by watery echoes. I said it again, louder. The woman turned toward me, her face a frighteningly rococo gold-cheeked carnival mask, permanently swollen with laughter. She nodded her head vigorously yes.

I put my gun back in my pocket and rushed forward. The mask was tied in back with a knotted silk ribbon, which I couldn't unthread with my gloved fingers. I pulled the mask off awkwardly over her head, and she gave a little cry of pain as it raked across her nose. "Sorry!" Underneath the mask, she was gagged with a red rubber ball gag held in place with a band of tight elastic. I grabbed the ball with one hand to protect Manon's teeth and pulled the elastic till it stretched enough to pass over her head.

Manon swallowed hard several times before she could summon enough saliva to form words. "Luke! Thank God. They're waiting farther up the tunnel."

"Who?"

She coughed and spit. "Bergé's men! There must be half a dozen of them."

"What about Harlequin?"

"How did you know?"

"Know what?"

"They're all in costumes. Just like this one. And masks!"

I turned her around and untied the knots around her wrists. "How did you get down here like this?"

"They made me climb down at gunpoint. They tied me up afterward."

"Hey! You're not stuttering!"

Her eyes sparkled. "I know! Come on."

I followed the lavishly costumed Manon directly into the blinding blue light of the tunnel. Séverine's mobile phone showed that it was already ten minutes after midnight. "We're late!" I pulled out the SIG Sauer.

"Where's the painting?" Manon hissed over her shoulder.

"Benoît has it. He's coming through a different tunnel."

She pulled up her petticoats to run. After only a few steps, the light in the tunnel went out and we were suddenly stumbling through pitch-blackness. Manon yelped and fell, and I tripped over her legs and fell on top of her. I threw my arms out to brace my fall, and the pistol went flying. I landed with Manon's shoulder in my ribs, and I twisted sideways into the sewage at the bottom of the tunnel. We lay panting for a moment.

"Are you all right?" I said.

"Yes." A sound like a giant butane torch filled the tunnels. "What do you think that is?"

"Water!" I said.

I scrambled to my feet, felt for Manon and helped her stand up, as well, but the moment we were both upright, a wall of water waist-high swept us back off our feet, and we were suddenly bobbing toward the Seine in a chute of foul runoff. I went under and then fought back to the surface, bits and pieces of things bobbing and bumping me in the dark. I spit and sputtered and grabbed onto Manon, who was trying to plant her feet against the surge. My right toe caught a stone, and I catapulted upright and nearly somersaulted over. We skidded backwards through the water, the full force of the muck flowing into my nose and mouth. My back smacked against the wall of an intersecting tunnel, and I dug my heels in behind me and pushed myself into the side tunnel at the crossroads. I grabbed Manon tightly around the waist with both arms and helped her right herself.

For another minute or so, we half-sat against the wall, holding onto each other, pinned by the flow of water. Then, gradually, the floodwaters receded, and the sewer returned to its former, relatively mild flow. However and wherever it had been blocked, it now ran freely again, knee-high, and I was able to get my bearings and stand upright. Manon shivered in my arms and burrowed into me for warmth, but we were both soaked through with the freezing snowmelt.

"You okay?" I said.

"Something's caught on my arm."

I felt down her shoulders. Her satin dress was filmed with grit and slime. I found a strap twisted around her left elbow. At first, I thought it was her ball gag, but I discovered, when my finger hit something hard and a light came on, that I was holding my own headlamp. I disentangled it from Manon's arm and put it on.

The light was fainter now and flickered. "We'd better get out of here."

I shone the light at the ceiling until I found the street signs above the tunnel intersection. Rue Francois the First and Cours la Reine: we had been washed to the other side of the Grand Palais! Manon's teeth chattered.

"Let's get some of those layers off of you and find a ladder to the surface."

I helped Manon strip down to a set of frilly bloomers, stained various ugly shades of gray, and then I shone the light all around the tunnel, hoping against hope to see rusted rungs nearby; but there was nothing overhead but pipes and insulated cables. I took a step up the rue Francois the First tunnel and played the light across the ceiling there. No luck.

A booming voice called, "You there! With the light!"

I recognized it immediately. "Benoît!"

"Luke?" I heard the splash of footsteps running toward us. "Where the hell have you been?"

"I have Manon. What about the painting?"

"I gave it to Harlequin! Didn't you see him?"

"No."

Benoît was utterly drenched in sewer water, and an unidentifiable black thing clung to his hair above his right ear. When he saw Manon in her dirty bloomers, he softened and petted her head fondly. "Let's get her out of here," he said.

"And Bergé's men?"

"They didn't show."

Manon unclenched her teeth. "No, they brought me." She was wracked by violent shivering spasms.

"Bergé's men brought you? I thought Harlequin had you!"

"It was Bergé. That's who dressed me in these clothes."

I looked at Benoît. "Was Bergé Harlequin?"

"Let's get back to the street," said Benoît. "We can sort this out later."

Benoît took my headlamp and led the way, and I walked behind Manon, so that she was safely between us. We waded upstream, toward a spot where Benoît remembered a manhole, at Avenue Franklin Roosevelt. He eventually found the rusty ladder he was looking for, and we climbed back up to the street.

We pushed the manhole cover away and emerged into the wintry night, where streetlamps turned the mounding snow the color of parchment. Manon was safe. We had gotten rid of the painting. As far as I knew, two and a half million euros were still waiting for us in Giselle's bank account. Except for the fact that we were soaked in freezing sewer water in a snowstorm, things could not have been better. So why did I feel so empty?

We walked toward the Champs-Élysées. It took just fifteen minutes until we saw the first flashing blue light. We were too tired and frozen to run. We just kept walking until the police cars pulled up beside us.

16

A Final Surprise

The police at the Les Halles Station let me shower—more for their own benefit, I thought, than mine—and gave me some preposterously large green coveralls to wear. Cleaned up, in my borrowed City of Paris garb, I looked like a miniature version of Benoît.

The smirking officer in charge of my case—who, I was beginning to believe, truly never slept—escorted me to an overheated office, where a police detective and officers from the BRB and RMN took turns questioning me. It felt almost like a panel conversation on a nighttime television chat show, since we talked more about personal theories than facts. I told them my belief, as clearly as I could articulate it, that Bergé had been behind the whole thing from the start; that, by demanding the painting from Bergé in the first place, Jacques Martin had triggered Bergé's insane jealousy; and that, by subsequently kidnapping Napoleon le Tigre in order to avoid a direct negotiation with Bergé, Martin had set off Bergé's insatiable lust for vengeance. The fact that Bergé possessed essentially unlimited financial means and a penchant for theatricality had only made Martin's position that much less tenable.

"You're saying that Bergé stole his own painting from the Grand Palais?" the BRB investigator said incredulously.

"I can't prove it."

"And that Bergé kidnapped you and someone named Napoleon le Tigre?"

"No, Jacques Martin kidnapped Napoleon le Tigre. Bergé kidnapped me and took me to his apartment on rue de Babylone. You can verify it: ask Bergé's chauffeur if he's had any accidents in the past day or so. Or check the local hospital records. Look for bullet holes in Bergé's apartment."

"Bullet holes from this gun that you lost in the sewer somewhere?"

"That's right. It's probably in the Seine by now, but maybe not. Maybe it's still in the tunnels under the Grand Palais. You could at least look."

"And tell me again, was it Martin or Bergé who kidnapped your girlfriend's daughter, dressed her in Italian Renaissance clothes and tied her up in the sewer?"

"That was Bergé. He wanted to make it look like a mysterious third party was involved in the ransom. That's what he's wanted the whole time, to make it look like someone else was behind everything, to throw us off. But it was always just Bergé."

The investigator said, "Bergé had to throw you off because he stole his own painting from the Grand Palais?"

"Exactly!"

"So that Jacques Martin wouldn't get the painting, even though Martin didn't have a legal claim to the painting to begin with?"

I sighed. "Well, he had this napkin." I realized that I had never actually seen the napkin that Martin's claim to the painting rested on. "Anyway, he *said* he had this napkin."

It did not really surprise me when, several hours into my interrogation, we all learned together that the police had received an anonymous tip about the location of *The Despair of Pierrot* and found it in Jacques Martin's apartment—hidden behind a framed poster of *The Despair of Pierrot* that was hanging on Martin's bedroom wall. The fact that the canvas had been draped over my own shower rod as recently as twelve hours before and that Jacques Martin had been in jail for more than thirty-six hours before that only made my Bergé revenge scenario more plausible, to my mind; but the detectives didn't see it that way. For them, all fingers pointed toward Martin, and since they had actually recovered the stolen canvas from his apartment, it was difficult to make a sound argument for any other solution.

The BRB investigator took the pen he had been using to record my testimony and flung it across the room. It bounced off the wall and spun harmlessly to the floor. "Another victory for the justice system," he said. He got up and left the room.

* * * * *

By the time they processed and released me, Manon and Benoît had already been sent home. I walked out of the police station onto rue aux Ours in my ridiculous green coveralls, which the police said they were going to bill me for. It felt anticlimactic, but I reminded myself of the massive amount of cash awaiting us in Giselle's Swiss bank account and felt much better.

The storm had passed. Icy patches of snow, black with grime, clung to the curbs, and the tops of the enshadowed cornices on the northern side of the streets were still rounded with white; but the avenues and sidewalks had been swept clean. The sun shone bright and cold.

Whatever had happened, however the painting had appeared in Jacques Martin's apartment, I imagined that now everyone could be reasonably happy with the outcome of the affair—everyone but Jacques Martin, of course. Today was the first day of the weekend-long auction at the Grand Palais, and *The Despair of Pierrot* would surely fetch a much higher price than it would have before all this drama, no doubt enough to cover the two and a half million euros that Bergé had paid out in ransom. The auction had become the nation's leading entertainment event for a couple of days, and Pierre Bergé had managed, in-between the time he had spent kidnapping people and orchestrating a major art theft from himself, to give a dozen interviews that beatified Yves Saint Laurent and lauded his concern for charitable organizations. The French police could crow about their efficiency—as far as the police were concerned, the theft itself had been solved, though no one had yet explained how the painting had been removed from the Grand Palais. And Jean-Pierre, Manon, Benoît, Séverine, Giselle and I had still managed to come out relatively unscathed and two and a half million euros richer. That deserved a celebration, so I dropped by the Happy Elephant for a snifter of vintage armagnac, hoping we could all compare notes on what had happened, and I could shake the feeling of letdown and malaise that followed me from the police station.

When I arrived at just after eleven in the morning, Giselle was sitting across the bar from Jean-Pierre. She jumped up, threw her arms around my neck and covered my face with kisses. "Nice outfit!" she said. "Are those Benoît's?"

I pulled the coveralls out to their full dimensions. "One size fits all. Where is everyone?"

"Manon is asleep at Giselle's," Jean-Pierre said. "She promised to come by when she wakes up. She's obviously had a hard couple of days. Benoît is who-knows-where. We haven't heard from Séverine since last night. But you may be interested to know that Joseph Danton stopped by this morning."

"Danton came to the Happy Elephant? Why?"

"He says he left you a thousand voicemails, and he needs to talk to you right away about *The Despair of Pierrot*."

I motioned for Jean-Pierre to put the Happy Elephant's

phone on the bar, and I dialed Danton's private mobile number. "Luke," he said, "I want you to know, up front, that I'm not going to ask any questions about how anything happened. I have my obligations to the RMN, but I also have other obligations, and I know how complicated the world can sometimes be."

"What are you talking about?"

"Pierre Bergé hasn't called you?"

"Why should he?"

"Frankly, I don't understand what I'm about to say, but I have a feeling that you might. Bergé called me this morning and pledged a sizeable donation to *L'Association des Amis du Congo*."

"What's so hard to understand about that?"

"He says he'll give the AAC ten times the amount of money that *The Despair of Pierrot* brings at auction, but only on one condition." Danton paused for so long that I thought the call had dropped.

"And what's the condition?"

"That the AAC receive a donation of two and a half million euros from you."

My heart sank. "From me? Where would I get two and a half million euros?"

"Indeed."

This was real blackmail: Bergé was trying to buy back his ransom money for charity! He was willing to pay ten times the value of the painting just to make sure that we didn't profit from it.

"You know I don't have that kind of money," I said unconvincingly. "You've been signing my paychecks for the last two years!"

"He says you have till the end of the auction tomorrow night to think about it, then the offer will be rescinded." Danton drew a breath. "Luke, again, I make no judgments, but let me say this: if it actually were within your power to do such a thing, you could literally save the lives of hundreds if not thousands of people. You know that all too well. Bergé is offering to turn your two and a half million—however you may have gotten it—into a vastly greater sum: ten times the price of the painting! Think of it. Think of all the children you've seen in the Congo living lives of despair, under the threat of violence. Think of the babies dying needlessly in their mothers' arms. You know how much that kind of aid would mean to them, to the people who have no other hope for a decent life. So I'm asking you to consider it. If, indeed, such a thing were possible."

I told him I'd call him back. I hung up and explained the deal to Giselle and Jean-Pierre.

"*Incroyable!*" Jean-Pierre said.

"He's buying his money back at such a premium and for such a good cause that it's impossible to say no."

Giselle said, "But what if you gave him back only two million, say? Would he donate ten times that amount to the AAC? We could still keep something for our trouble."

I called Danton back immediately, and he said that Bergé had anticipated this question and the donation had to be exactly two and a half million, no more, no less. He was going to let us keep the money only by taking food and medicine away from starving women and children in refugee camps. Bergé was diabolical.

"What I don't understand," said Jean-Pierre, "is how that painting could have ended up in Jacques Martin's apartment. Was Martin really Harlequin after all?"

"No," I said. "He was in prison when that deal was arranged. And he was also a dupe in the exchange at Les Frigos. Somebody else had to be Harlequin. Someone who knew about Les Frigos, who knew Séverine was involved, who knew that Napoleon le Tigre and Benoît were the same person. The only person who could know all that is Bergé."

"You think he was also the one who threw the brick through Séverine's shop window?"

"He had just been there ten minutes before, and he was the only one who knew that I was connected to both Séverine and Napoleon le Tigre. It had to be him—or one of his henchmen."

* * * * *

We spent the next hour flipping between radio stations on the Happy Elephant's stereo system, listening to reports of the theft and recovery of *The Despair of Pierrot*. As if the name Yves Saint Laurent and all the well-known works of art in the auction weren't enough, the gossips and news readers now had dozens more angles to cover: in the relationship between Jacques Martin and Yves Saint Laurent; in the salacious sexual underworld of the 1970s fashion scene; in the disputatious nature of Pierre Bergé, the ruthless tycoon behind the ultimate success of Saint Laurent. And since the auction was set to start that very afternoon, commentators could milk every gavel strike, play up every bidding war for every artwork, cut away from the auction to police updates and news flashes and further scandalous gossip throughout the day. Most of the chatter revolved around how Jacques Martin could have masterminded the whole scheme and left behind no clues at the Grand Palais: his guilt was assumed—after all, he had demanded the painting from Bergé, kidnapped a man, shot into a crowd at Les Frigos, and *Pierrot* had ultimately been recovered from his apartment—these were all known facts. But we at the Happy Elephant knew that Martin simply could not have done it. The only person unaccounted for was the mysterious Harlequin, and we awaited only the arrival of

Manon to confirm our suspicions and put the final touches to the story.

Manon ran into the Happy Elephant at just after noon, wearing her typical faded jeans and ratty sweater, quite a pleasant change from the garish costume she had been wearing the night before in the sewer. After a round of hugs and kisses and assurances that she was all right, Giselle burst out, "Who was it? Who was Harlequin?"

"Harlequin?" Manon was taken aback. "He was the clown who always ended up with Columbina."

"Not in Commedia dell'Arte," I said. "The one who kidnapped you. The one who held you for ransom and put that costume on you!"

"Like I said before, it was Bergé. He made me wear that costume and forced me to climb into the sewer," Manon said. "Bergé was Harlequin."

Giselle's mouth was hanging open. "Darling, you're not stuttering."

Manon beamed. "I know! Isn't it wonderful!"

"But how?"

"I don't know. Bergé drugged me, and when I woke up, I was wearing a stage costume and I could speak perfectly normally. I'm so happy!" She threw herself into her mother's arms.

* * * * *

While we waited for Benoît and Séverine to arrive, we heard Manon's tale, which was simple enough. She had been pursued almost immediately upon leaving Les Frigos, not by the police but by a sleek black Maybach, the super-luxury high-performance sports car line of Mercedes-Benz. "The funny thing is," Manon said, "I had never even seen a Maybach in person before, but I recognized it because my friend Beatrice and I had just done a report for university analyzing wealth disproportions between social classes in the twenty-first century." Manon then began a Marxist diatribe against luxury cars, which would have made sense if she herself didn't drive a BMW Z8. After some political analysis of French income brackets, we reined Manon back into her story. "I couldn't shake the Maybach," said Manon. "I could lose it for a period of time with some clever switchbacks or just good luck, but it was like they had a homing device on me, because every time I would get free, they would find me again within half an hour."

Jean-Pierre suggested, "Maybe there was a tracking beacon in the painting."

"Or in the frame," I suggested.

"Yes, possibly in the frame," Manon said. "I cut the canvas completely out of the frame only when I stuck it in the picnic basket at Dalloyau. And then I put the empty frame back in my car, and they found me again!"

"And they didn't track the canvas to my apartment. It would be easier to hide an electronic device in the frame than on the canvas."

During the brief moment when Manon had lost her pursuers near the Luxembourg Gardens, she had ducked into Dalloyau and bought the gift basket, taken it out to her car and repacked it with the canvas, and then returned it to the shop for delivery, yet her pursuers in the Maybach were soon on her again. "However they did it, they were savvy enough to keep finding my car and staying after me. But once I'd gotten rid of the canvas, there was no reason to keep running, so I just put my car in a carpark and ran. Near the Bois de Boulogne, I saw some pylons set up around an open manhole, and I thought of *Les Miserables*, so I just climbed down, but they caught me pretty quickly."

"Who?"

"Two really good-looking guys wearing Yves Saint Laurent suits. They took me to Bergé's apartment."

I asked, "Were these guys really young and sleek and looked like models?"

"Yes!"

"Were they listening to the Pet Shop Boys in the car?"

"No, George Michael."

"I knew it."

"I think he got the idea for the rendezvous in the sewers from me," Manon continued. "We talked at some length about *Les Miserables* after his men had dressed me in that ridiculous costume. Bergé actually knows quite a lot about Victor Hugo, and Commedia dell'Arte, and lots of things. He's sort of charming."

"Manon," I said. "He kidnapped you, drugged you and held you for ransom."

"But he didn't hurt me," Manon said. "And I've stopped stuttering." She could see by the look on my face that I was not happy with her complacent attitude. "It's a complicated situation, Luke."

* * * * *

Benoît arrived next, and he threw his two cents in about Bergé. "It makes sense," he said. "Bergé would do anything to spite one of Yves' lovers. I believe that. And he's also rich enough and resourceful enough to pay some city worker to divert the sewer temporarily. It wouldn't even be difficult mechanically—they do it all the time during construction projects. You'd just have to pay someone enough to keep quiet about it later, and he could."

"But why? Why would you do that?"

Benoît said, "As much as Yves Saint Laurent deserves the credit for the fashion designs, Bergé was the one who made all that money for him, and Bergé was an artist, too. I told you what he did for my career. He's organized art shows and happenings and public installations for years." Jean-Pierre poured him a glass of red wine. "Why not? A Commedia dell'Arte performance in the sewers. It's not the worst idea in the world. It's a metaphor, maybe."

"You think dressing up an actual hostage in Renaissance costumes and taking her into the sewers is a kind of performance?"

"It's certainly a kind of performance, Luke."

"No, it isn't! It was a hostage ransom."

Benoît rolled his eyes. "It doesn't have to be on a canvas to be art, you know."

I almost thought he was going to argue that, at Les Frigos, he had actually been a piece of sculpture and not a real hostage. Everything, it seemed, could be turned into a philosophical abstraction or an aesthetic statement.

I said, "Ask Jacques Martin if he thinks it's art. He's in a real prison."

Benoît conceded. "Art has more real-life consequences for some than for others. But Martin went looking for trouble. To declare openly that Yves Saint Laurent had promised him one of Bergé's priceless paintings as a token of love, with no real evidence? Martin must have been a little crazy to start with."

"All this was Martin's fault?" I said. "That sounds like blaming the victim."

"Martin was just lovesick," Manon said. "Lovesick and grieving for Yves' death, and it made him lose control."

"You know," said Jean-Pierre. "If Bergé was the one who set up the exchange at Les Frigos, he probably wanted to frame Martin there, to let the cops catch Martin with the painting that night. But you and Manon fouled it up, so he had to do it all over again. The whole Harlequin act was probably improvised."

The theory was tidy enough, I supposed, in that it accounted for all the mysteries, except one: how had Bergé removed the painting from the Grand Palais itself?

"He had access to it," Manon said. "And he could have gone in late at night, perhaps when there was only one guard or two, paid them off. The surveillance camera freezes for a moment, Bergé walks out with his own painting, the guards get a million each. You can imagine it easily enough."

I shook my head. "But why take such extraordinary risks, when Martin probably didn't have a legal claim to the painting to begin with?"

"Love," Giselle and Jean-Pierre said together, at exactly the same moment Benoît said, "Revenge."

As this chorus of love and revenge reverberated through the Happy Elephant, Séverine appeared at the door. She was beaming. She held up her left hand and there, on her fourth finger, was a silver band encrusted with diamonds, which caught the meager winter light and scattered it prismatically around the bar.

"Congratulate me," Séverine said. "Eugene and I just got married!"

My jaw dropped. In my mind, I replayed the recording she had made for me, the fantasy she had described, the sexual act she had performed for me, and the night we had just spent together in her apartment, when she had tried to seduce me.

"Congratulations," we all said, each of us dumbfounded in our own private ways.

17

Un/Complicated

The auction proceeded as planned, minus *The Despair of Pierrot*. The canvas itself had to be re-authenticated by appraisers before Christie's could offer it for bidding, but the rest of the pieces garnered a record three hundred seventy-three million euros—half a billion dollars!—all of which Bergé donated to various charities.

Once *The Despair of Pierrot* was recertified, remounted and reframed, it was sold as a stand-alone piece at a special auction two days after the main event. Because of its new international renown, it fetched nearly five million euros, the most ever for a work by James Ensor; and, because we agreed to donate the two and a half million that Bergé had paid us as ransom, Joseph Danton received wire transfers the next day for nearly fifty-three million euros. My only stipulation to the deal was that our donation be booked to Bergé, since we couldn't afford the tax inquiry, and Bergé and Danton agreed. Because Bergé's huge gift had depended entirely on my two and a half million, I told Danton that I had technically become the AAC's most important donor, though no one would ever know it but him.

"That's why you'd make such a valuable asset to our organization, Luke," said Danton. "Because you understand how fundraising really works."

Jacques Martin was eventually tried and convicted of a dozen different crimes, the most serious of which involved firing his gun into the crowd at Les Frigos and possessing the stolen canvas of *The Despair of Pierrot*. He was sentenced to thirty-seven years in prison—at his age, essentially a life sentence. The trial did not reveal how the painting had gotten into Martin's apartment, and no one ever discovered how it was taken from the Grand Palais in the first place. My friends all believed that Pierre Bergé had engineered both events, that he had masterminded the whole caper to punish Martin for loving Yves Saint Laurent.

But Martin simply could not compete with Bergé, and Bergé had gone to extraordinary lengths to make sure he knew it—such extraordinary lengths that I could only suppose that Yves Saint Laurent's love for Martin had been powerful and real and that Bergé knew it. For every Pierrot in this life, I thought, there would always be a Harlequin to put him in his place, and there would always be a Columbina to fight over, whether Columbina was a girl or a boy, young or old, rich or poor.

* * * * *

The day after the special auction of *The Despair of Pierrot*, Jean-Pierre hosted a celebration of Séverine's marriage at the Happy Elephant. Giselle and Manon tacked meters and meters of red and white tulle to the walls, in great swoops and swirls. The bar itself and all the tables were covered with plain white tablecloths, and atop the bar a line of champagne glasses soldiered toward a *croquembouche*—a typical French wedding cake, made of a high cone of profiteroles held together with caramel sauce, decorated with candied almonds. Jean-Pierre had programmed his stereo to play songs that he knew Séverine liked, and just now Dinah Washington's "Baby, You've Got What It Takes" was sassing up the bar.

Eugene and his friends crowded in and drank and laughed.

Most of his friends were colleagues from the French Clinical Biological Agency, and Eugene had already hosted a separate wedding celebration for his family at the extremely upscale Mon Vieil Ami restaurant on Île-Saint-Louis: the Happy Elephant was obviously a huge step down from Eugene's usual haunts, and he acted like he was doing Séverine a favor by appearing in such an obviously mediocre place, but he did not turn his nose up at Jean-Pierre's wine selection. Benoît was the life of the party, telling tales of his days as Napoleon le Tigre that he had kept to himself all these years, and his connection to Yves Saint Laurent titillated the crowd; and Manon was chattering on and on with anyone who would listen—she had not stopped talking since she'd lost her stutter, and her eyes shimmered and sparkled when she spoke.

As we drank and danced, I thought of Jacques Martin in his prison cell, and Pierre Bergé, ruthless and vengeful and free. As a result of the Yves Saint Laurent auction, Bergé had become Europe's greatest private philanthropist, and he had cemented his stature as the brilliant, generous husband of Saint Laurent—the strength behind France's most celebrated and influential fashion genius.

As our celebration was winding down, and we were emptying the last bottles of Krug Grand Cuvée, I cornered Séverine alone at the back of the bar. She was drunk and theatrically happy.

"I listened to the recording you made," I said.

"Good."

"Why are you doing this?"

"What do you mean?"

"You tell me you want to do all of these kinky things with me and get back together with me, and the next day you marry Eugene?"

"You don't want to be with me," Séverine said. "You told

me so."

"So why did you make that recording?"

"Because it's true. It's all true. And you don't get to leave me like you did. You just don't."

"You don't feel embarrassed at all by the things you said, or did?"

"Why should I?"

"Don't you think Eugene would be embarrassed? Or feel betrayed?"

"What happened between you and me has nothing to do with Eugene." She leaned in toward me. "Just like it has nothing to do with Giselle. You know, you really hurt me and left everything unfinished between us because you thought that leaving me had to do with Giselle. But it didn't. You always get things mixed up." She took my arm and led me toward the bar, where Eugene was pouring a final round of champagne. "And," she whispered in my ear, "if you'd ever like to try any of those things I told you about on that recording, you know where to find me." She winked.

I joined Giselle and Manon at the bar, and we all toasted the happy couple, who did indeed look very happy. It was a complicated happiness.

That night, safely back in my apartment once again, Giselle and I made love, without costumes, props, whips, gags or handcuffs. It was not complicated at all.

www.ingramcontent.com/pod-product-compliance
Lightning Source LLC
Chambersburg PA
CBHW020631250626
47154CB00008B/2622